You Forgot the Sauce

An Alzheimer's Journey

You Won't Forget

Copyright

CONTENTS

Brotherly Love

Chapter 1

August 2013

Dr Steven Iffinger was driving his BMW M3 with uncharacteristic care along the winding country road heading towards Leura in the Blue Mountains, a couple of hours out of Sydney, Australia. He was listening to John Mayer, his elder brother's favourite singer. The mobile phone rang disrupting his daydreaming; frustrated, he answered the phone using his free hands. It was his surgery.

'Doctor, we have an emergency. There's been a train crash and they're calling for all available medical services. Are you nearby?' the practice manager asked.

'No, I'm at least two hours away. I'm in the Blue Mountains.'

'What's happened?'

'A north bound train has derailed and we believe three carriages have rolled down an embankment.'

'Have you got any idea if people have been killed?'

'Not at this stage, Doctor, although from the television pictures coming in it would be a miracle if there weren't some deaths.'

'I'll try and get there as soon as I can. What station is the closest?'

'Granville.'

'Oh my God, not again.'

Steven hung up and tried to get the train crash out of his mind, trying not to feel guilty.

'I didn't know there was going to be a bloody train crash,' he thought.

'If I can't manage a couple of hours away from the fucking practice I should give the whole thing away...No, I'm a doctor, I need to be there. I'll have to make this visit a short one.'

He turned up the volume on John Mayer again and continued his journey, eventually reaching his destination, "Blue Haven Nursing Home".

He parked the car and approached the entrance, hoping Dr Russell was on duty. He was.

'James, I was hoping I would see you.'

'Hello, Steven, how's life with you?'

'I just got word there's been a serious train derailment, so I need to get back as soon as possible. Still, I need to see him.'

'OK, I guess you would like an update.'

'Yes, if I could.'

'Why don't we go into my office? It's more private.'

The two men walked down the wide corridor until they reached Dr. Russell's office.

'So how's he behaving himself?'

'He's no trouble, Steven, he keeps to himself a lot as you know.'

'Has he deteriorated since my last visit?'

'I take it he is still on Razadyne®?'

'We've had to strengthen his medicine to Namenda®. As you know, regulating glutamate levels is essential when the disease becomes more severe.

'When did you last visit him?'

'Three weeks ago. I try and get here every week but I had to attend a medical conference in Boston.'

'OK, well I would have to say that he is having trouble recognising the nursing staff. As for me, he doesn't have a clue who I am.'

'That's disappointing news. Does he still steal stuff?'

'I believe there is a shortage of spoons in the kitchen, God knows where he hides them but the staff can't find any for love or money. They think he buries them when he goes out in the grounds for his daily walk.'

'Is there any way of knowing how long he's got?'

'Hard to tell, Steve, it could be a year or two. Then again, it could be a lot sooner. As you know, this insidious condition is unpredictable.'

'Thanks, James, I appreciate your frankness. Can I see him now please?'

'Of course. You know where to find him.'

Steve walked down to the dementia ward, he pressed in the code to the lock and entered. There were people walking around with various levels of dementia. Some looked perfectly normal, while others were just shuffling along with vacant looks. It was difficult not to stare but he knew that would be the wrong thing to do. He entered the television lounge where he knew he would find his patient. Sure enough, sitting in the recliner watching André Rieu was the man he had come to visit. He sat next to him and endeavoured to get his attention. He looked at Steve and turned back to André. Steve knew that he would have no hope capturing his patient's attention until the concert reached its climactic finish.

Finally the DVD stopped.

'Do you want to go for a walk?'

'Yes, that would be good. Are you going to be warm enough? It's a bit nippy out there today.'

'I don't have a coat.'

'Let me see if I can find one for you, mate.'

Steven went to his room and grabbed a coat, one of three that he possessed.

'Here you go, mate, put this on.'

He didn't question where Steve had obtained the coat. He just put it on and headed for the exit and out into the grounds.

They walked amongst the pine trees and admired the views over the valley and the mountains beyond. Steven knew that conversation was futile but nevertheless spoke about his wife, Natalie, and how his boys were going at school. He even got stuck into the State Government about their commitment to infrastructure-spending. The man just walked in silence.

The two men arrived back at the main building just in time for dinner; Steven took him into the dining room and sat him down at his usual table. Sitting with him was Rebecca, aged sixty, a former ballerina who had danced all over the world including in Russia with the Bolshoi. Next to her was Russell, a former lawyer, and Nancy who had been a housewife all her life. Yet to join them was Frank, a former interstate truck driver. A very diverse group with one thing in common: dementia.

Steven bade his patient farewell promising to visit him again the following week.

He left the nursing home with the same thoughts he always had: 'How could this happen to this man, of all people?'

Steven began the two-hour drive home in silence. He was lost in his own world.

> 'To think the man he had just left was at the height of his profession on the brink of discovering a cure that would change people's lives. Life just wasn't fair.'

Steve drove the Beema as fast as he knew he could get away with; if the police stopped him, he was sure they'd understand. He had to get to Granville as quickly as possible.

The journey took an hour and a half. He parked the car as close to the site of the accident as possible. He grabbed his bag and hurried over, looking for any other medical personnel Steve recognised a work colleague and approached her.

> 'Helen Hi, what's the situation?'

'Oh hi, Steve, it's pretty bad. The Fire Brigade believe there are up to thirty people still trapped. We can't get to them until the SES can cut them out.'

'So we have to wait until we can safely get to them?'

'That's about it.'

The chilling sounds of screaming and crying were overpowering. The haunting sound of trapped people crying for help deeply affected the two doctors. They had to get these victims out.

Just then the head of the State Emergency Services (SES) approached the two doctors.

'Doctors, we have a situation where a young girl is trapped with a beam crushing her arm. There is a smell of gas around so we dare not use the oxy acetylene to try and cut her free. We need your help to get her out.'

'You better show us where she is' said Steve with a degree of apprehension in his voice.'

The three scrambled over the bent and twisted carriages until they reached the carriage where the girl was trapped. The two doctors crawled in; she must have been about twelve or thirteen years old. After examining her they detected a faint pulse but if she wasn't freed soon, she would die: a decision had to be made; the only way this girl could be saved was to amputate her left arm above the elbow.

Steve would perform the amputation and Helen would act as anaesthetist while monitoring her vital signs. He had performed amputations before but they were the clean sterile conditions of a hospital operating theatre. After an hour the young girl had been freed and taken by ambulance to Prince Alfred Hospital

The two doctors remained on site for the next sixteen hours and in that time were required to perform three more amputations and treat several heart attack victims.

At the end of the day the casualty count was forty-one passengers. Ten people had died on the scene.

"This will be the place for a village"

John Batman

Founder of Melbourne, Australia

Chapter 2

Steve arrived at his Woollahra terrace at about 11am the next morning despite the hour he poured himself a malt scotch, his favourite, MacCallum's 18 year old and slumped down into the lounge and thought about the day he had just had. This is what he trained for but no amount of training could prepare you for the injuries seen in a train wreck.

Steve looked at his watch, it was twelve noon he could snatch fours sleep before the kids got home from school. Kate, his wife wouldn't get home until six.

He lied in the bed tossing and turning he couldn't get the images out of his head images he hoped would never be experienced again. Unfortunately in his profession the chances were high. He eventually nodded off.

Jonathon and Rebecca came home, realising their father was home sleeping, they left him alone. It wasn't until Kate arrived home did he rise and go out into the kitchen.

'Tough day darling?' Kate asked.

'Sure was, very tough.'

'I knew when you called me that the chances of you getting home last night would be remote.'

'We didn't stop, couldn't stop until the last of the injured were freed.'

'It must have been horrible.'

'The worst injuries I've ever witnessed.'

'Oh dear.'

'Changing the subject how was your visit to Blue Haven?'

'Distressing I'm afraid.'

'Such a brilliant man, it's so sad.'

'Alzheimer's can hit anyone it doesn't differentiate between scientists or politicians.'

The family sat down to their evening meal and had the normal family conversations.

'Hey Dad guess what?'

'I don't know mate what?'

'I got picked for the firsts in the cricket team.'

'Well done I'll have to make time to come and see you play. When's your next match?'

'Next Wednesday at Brighton Grammar, I think play begins at 2pm.'

'Well at this stage I should be able to come along.'

'I hope so.'

'You don't sound too hopeful.'

'Well you've missed most of the matches you said you'd attend.'

'Now Jon your father would only miss a match because of a medical emergency, be fair.'

'Sorry.'

'Does anybody here want to hear how my day went?' scowled Rebecca.

'Of course darling what happen at school today?' Steve inquired.

'Nothing, absolutely nothing.'

The other three just looked at each other.

After dinner Jonathon and Rebecca went off to do their homework. Kate and Steve retired to the living room and watched television. Steve couldn't keep his eyes open so they went to bed.

Brighton Melbourne 1987

Steve was riding his bicycle along South Road on his way home to Bentleigh. It was always an enjoyable ride on a Friday afternoon, no homework and the weekend approaching. He started to descend a steep hill he changed gears and began riding as fast as he could. By his reckoning he must have been going thirty kilometres an hour but it was probably closer to twenty. A car swerved in front of him not seeing the young schoolboy on a bike. Steve was pushed into the curb the bike crashed into a tree. Steve was thrown over the handlebars and hit a brick wall in front of a large house. He could hear the crack before he even fell back onto the pavement his leg was badly broken.

The driver of the car raced over to him to see if he could be of some assistance, the woman who lived in the house asked if she could ring an ambulance. The driver of the car agreed that she should. An ambulance arrived within ten minutes the ambos examined Steve's leg, they carefully placed Steve onto the gurney and slid him into the ambulance all the while reassuring the young schoolboy.

The ambulance sped him to Brighton Private Hospital where they assessed the break with X-rays. It was decided to operate and insert some screws into the bone.

Steve stayed in hospital for five days it was an experience that would determine his future career. The doctor who had operated on him visited him every day. The nurses who cared for him were fantastic. From that point on Steve decided he wanted to become a doctor.

After he was discharged from hospital he was restricted in his movements, the plaster on his leg was to remain for six to eight weeks. With the aid of crutches he could get around slowly. He returned to school, Haileybury College in Brighton. As a boy who had been so active in sports and such he became very frustrated.

His elder brother Robert was considered an academic he was awarded dux of his class each year and everybody including his teachers and fellow students expected him to become dux of the school in his final year.

Robert did have other interests outside the classroom, he was school tennis captain and captain of the chess team. Despite their obvious differences in age and interests the two Iffinger boys got on well.

Rob invited Steve to join the chess team seeing he wasn't going to be playing cricket or basketball for a while.

Steve accepted the invitation as a welcome diversion from schoolwork and utter boredom.

Rob and Steve played at home on occasion and it wasn't always Rob who won.

Steve enjoyed his tenure on the chess team and won his fair share of matches but when the plaster was finally removed and the doctors gave him the go ahead he was back playing cricket and basketball. The end of the season was looming and with that the beginning of the football season.

One thing had changed for Steve; he now made himself a commitment to devote himself to his studies to ensure that his grades would be high enough to enter Medical School at Melbourne University. He had two more years of secondary school to achieve his goal.

He knew it would take a real commitment but he also knew that sport would also play a big part in his school life.

Steve also had a wicked sense of humour, one morning the history teacher Mr Pitts drove up to the teachers car park in his brand new "Smart Car" it certainly drew the attention of the students and the other teachers. He proudly showed off the little car boasting fuel economy of four litres per one hundred kilometres.

The siren sounded and teachers and students found their appropriate classrooms.

Steve got together three of his best mates and they hatched a cunning plan. They would sneak out to the car park at lunchtime and lift up the Smart Car and hide it behind the shelter sheds.

They accomplished their mission without damaging Mr Pitts pride and joy.

At the end of the school day they hid waiting for Pitts to come out and proceed to the car park.

He walked up and down the car park several times before going to the Head Master's office to report the theft and call the police.

The boys had arranged to have an envelope delivered to the headmaster's office addressed to Pitts giving him instructions as to where the car could be found.

Most of the kids knew what had happened, they saw it happen but not one student razzed on the four perpetrators.

One other prank Steve orchestrated was played on the music teacher Mr Thring. Thring would quite often go to the toilet in the junior school where the pans were half the size as normal. He was a big man so it became a mystery to the senior school students.

One day they watched for Thring's regular visit sure enough, he entered the toilet block and chose a cubicle. Steve and his good mate Dave Quirk sneaked in looked under the doors of the cubicles identifying Thring by the size ten shoes. They threw a large firecracker under the door, the thing exploded, Thring jumped up a mile and landed down on the small toilet smashing the ceramic pan with his arse.

They had no intention of injuring him but the music teacher had six stitches in his left cheek. They ran like hell and got away with it. If they hadn't they would have been suspended.

School for the two brothers went without incident for the next two years. Steve decided he better stop the practical jokes; he didn't want to be expelled. Rob just carried on as usual until speech night of his final year it was announced that he had been awarded Dux of the School.

Rob decided to enrol for a science degree at Melbourne University knowing that once he graduated he needed to complete a Ph.D. in biological science if he was to follow his chosen career as a medical research scientist.

His ambition was to help try and find a cure for Alzheimer's the disease that took his Grandmother.

The Dementia Research Centre (DRC) in Sydney had already interviewed him. This research centre was regarded one of the best in Australia although it would mean a transfer to Sydney when he completed his PHD.

They gave Rob some background information.

Medical research scientists devise and conduct experiments in order to increase the body of scientific knowledge on topics related to medicine. They also develop new, or improve existing, drugs, treatments or other medically related products.

Medical research takes place in higher education institutions, research institutes, hospitals and industry. The level of research may be basic and involve investigating the underlying basis of health or disease or it may be more applied and include conducting clinical research, investigating methods of prevention, diagnosis and treatment of human disorders.

Research may be at the molecular level, carried out using appropriate cell and animal models, or human volunteers may be used to study the clinical effects of various factors.

Typical work activities

The specifics of the role vary according to the setting, but much of the work is laboratory-based. Tasks typically include:

Planning and conducting experiments and analysing or interpreting the results;

Keeping accurate records of work undertaken;

using specialist computer software to analyse data and to produce diagrammatic representation of results;

Teaching and supervising students (in higher education);

Writing and submitting applications and progress reports to funding bodies that support medical research (outside industry);

Discussing research progress with other departments, e.g. production and marketing (in industry);

Constantly considering the profit/loss potential of research products (in industry);

Collaborating with industry, research institutes, hospitals and academia.

Medical research scientists are also concerned with disseminating the results of their work to others. This includes:

Sharing the results of research with colleagues through presentations or discussions at team meetings;

Preparing presentations and delivering these at national and international scientific conferences;

Writing original papers for publication in peer-reviewed medical or scientific journals. (In industry, there is usually less pressure to publish.)

Scientists also need to keep up to date with other research being carried out in, or related to, their field of study. Activities that enable them to stay in touch with developments and advances in their field include:

Reading relevant scientific literature and journals;

Attending scientific meetings and conferences in order to hear presentations from other researchers and participate in informal discussions with scientists from other parts of the world.

Rob had seven years of University to look forward to.

At the beginning of his third year another Iffinger began his university journey, Steve began his five-year degree in medicine.

Rob showed Steve around the campus and introduced him to his group of friends. Once the first semester had finished Steve had established his own network of friends and had joined the University cricket team. He intended to try out for the football team when the season began. To Rob's astonishment Steve also joined the University Chess Club.

Melbourne University contains the cream of Australia

Rich and Thick.
Chapter 3

Steve also joined the Footlights Club he always fancied himself as a bit of a thespian.

His first skit in the University Review called "I've Got One of Those" was playing a British army Captain who was conducting his first execution on the Western Front.

Captain Smithers: Right prisoner you have been found guilty of desertion and sentenced to death by firing squad which is why all these soldiers are here standing in front of you with loaded Enfield 303s.

Prisoner: I wasn't deserting I just nicked out the back for a wee and lost my way.

Captain Smithers: Well it doesn't matter you've been found guilty and that's that.

Place the blindfold on the prisoner.

Prisoner: I wish you'd call me by my name its Percy Percival.

Captain Smithers: Sorry that's against regulations. If we all thought of you as Percy we might get too close to you and have trouble executing our duty as it were.

Prisoner: I can see you all, this blindfold is transparent!

Captain Smithers: Get him another blindfold!

(A new blindfold is tied)

Captain Smithers: Is it OK now!

Prisoner: If I like bend my head back I can see you through the slit. You're going to have to make it tighter.

(The blindfold is made tight)

Captain Smithers: Is it OK now!

Prisoner: It's too tight now it's very uncomfortable.

(The blindfold is removed)

Captain Smithers: Is it OK now!

Prisoner: Gee, I'm not too sure the sun is shining in my eyes. I can't see anyone! Would it be too much trouble to get me a cap?

May I make a suggestion?

Captain Smithers: What is it?

Prisoner: I think it would be easier for everybody concerned to execute people at night.

Captain Smithers: I'll mention it to HQ when we are finished shooting you.

Prisoner: Thank you just let them know where the suggestion came from. I should be given the credit.

(A cap is given to the prisoner)

Prisoner: Hello everybody, I can see you all clearly now. Oh dear those two soldiers have mud on their boots.

Captain Smithers: Men, this is not good enough we are the King's soldiers quickly go and clean your boots.

The two soldiers returned five minutes later.

Prisoner: Now that's better, looking good.

I must admit standing here with all those guns pointing at is a bit off putting.

Captain Smithers: Do you want to be blindfolded?

Prisoner: No thank you, how's this for a suggestion why don't I face the wall. That kills two birds with one stone, I won't need the cap and I won't be scared looking at the rifles

(The prisoner turns to the wall)

Captain Smithers: OK! Are we ready!

Prisoner: Hold on, it might portray me as a coward being shot in the back. I know, I think I'll face sideways and try not to look towards the soldiers!

(The prisoner stands sideways)

Captain Smithers: As you wish!

Firing Squad Member: Sir, its hard enough shooting young Percy here without making the shot more difficult.

Captain Smithers: Yes, I see your point. Firing Squad step forward three paces.

Firing Squad Member: We still have a problem with the angle sir.

Captain Smithers: Yes, I see well move together that should solve the problem.

Firing Squad Member: Not too close we're not Nancy boys.

Captain Smithers: Percy can you move a little to the left? That way we can hit you for sure!

Prisoner: Your left or mine!

Captain Smithers: My left, you're right!

Prisoner: How much?

Captain Smithers: Just one-step more towards the right and you are all set!

Prisoner (moves one step right): Is this good?

Captain Smithers: That's just perfect. Thanks so much for your cooperation. This is our first execution and we are trying to make it spot on. We are all a little nervous though.

Prisoner: You're nervous how do you think I feel? This is my first execution as well.

Captain Smithers: Do you have any last minute request?

Prisoner: Well as a matter of fact I'd rather fancy being part of your firing squad!

Captain Smithers: You are! You are the first person this squad has ever executed! You will always be a part of our lives. You will always be held fond in our memories. Isn't that right fellows?

Firing Squad: Three cheers for Percy. Hip Hip Hooray!

Prisoner: That's very nice but you all won't be a part of my life, I'll be dead! Now that's not fair?

Soldiers: Not fair! Not fair!

Prisoner: Then!

Soldiers: Release him! Release him!

Captain Smithers: All right lads if we release young Percy here who I know we have all grown very attached to; who are we going to shoot? We have to shoot someone or questions will be asked.

One soldier: I know we could go down to the cells and promise a slap up feast in the courtyard to the first prisoner who puts his hand up. That should do the trick.

Soldiers: Release him!

Captain Smithers: OK! But you better have somebody here to shoot in the next fifteen minutes

Captain Smithers: OK! Percy my boy you are free. You can join our firing squad! Now you can shoot anyone you want and government will pay you for it!

Prisoner: Thank you Sir! I'm really looking forward to it.

The review was hailed as a success and Steve enjoyed his starring role. He wasn't going to win an Academy Award for his performance but for a first time actor he performed very well.

Rob attended and got a real kick out of seeing his younger brother dressed as a British officer with a very convincing English accent treading the boards.

'I had no idea you were interested in acting mate. When did you start to get interested?'

'When I found out the ratio was four girls to one guy in the theatre company.'

'Oh Of course, I knew it couldn't be for the cultural enlightenment; you just wanted to score.'

'You got it in one brother.'

The conversation ended when the brother's parents joined them, it was a real bonus having them there as they were rarely in Melbourne let alone the country these days.

John was Managing Director of a large multi national drug company while his mother practiced commercial law. When her husband was appointed as CEO of Pfizer she resigned to support and travel with him. She had achieved all she could as a partner in Baker Wilson and felt it was the right thing to do.

After the show they all got together as a restaurant in Carlton and had a light supper.

'I really enjoyed your skit Steve who wrote it?' asked his father.

'Myself and a mate, he was Percy.'

'So the authors made sure they got the lead roles.'

'Absolutely.'

'We have something to tell you guys.' Announced their mother, Bev.

'Right, what?' asked Rob.

'We are moving to Sydney your father has been asked to take on South East Asia and the Pacific on top of Australia.'

'That's great but why Sydney?'

'The Board feels it would be the appropriate move.'

'So when's all this happening?' asked Steve.

'Next month.'

'Bloody hell they don't give you much notice do they?'

'No I'm afraid not.' John conceded.

'So I guess Steve and I will be looking for new digs?'

'No, not if you don't want to we would love you guys to stay in the house.'

'Really well that would be my choice. What about you Steve?'

'Yes mate, that would be great.'

'Just make sure there's a spare room available when your mother and I visit Melbourne.'

'Of course.' They both said laughing.

The house was a Tudor style two story in Toorak a very posh suburb. It had a swimming pool, a billiard room and a wine cellar; all the things a young university student would need.

'Just one thing boys I'm locking the wine cellar and taking the keys with me. Not that I don't trust you but it's taken years to build up my collection.'

'Sure Dad we understand.' Said Steve trying to sound sincere.

John and Bev were due to move into their Kirribilli apartment overlooking the harbour and the Sydney Opera House by 1 September, which worked well for Steve and Rob. They didn't actually have to do much as they were all ready living there. Never the less they had a three-week break from Uni to grow a customised to their newfound freedom.

The first task was to compile a guest list for the house warming party. They were not going to have a large party where uninvited residents would trash the place, just their closest friends.

The party was booked for 1st of October and all going to plan about forty residents would turn up.

The party was a great success and apart from some skinny-dipping in the pool it was a reasonably conservative affair with not too much dope smoked or alcohol consumed.

Next day the clean up began with the aid of a few sleepovers including Steve's girlfriend.

The remainder of the year went without incident and by the time end of year exams came and went both brothers passed with flying colours.

Not That There's Any Thing Wrong With That

Chapter 4

Steve was sitting on the couch watching television when Rob and his good mate, Andy, walked in and sat down.

'What are you watching mate?'

'A documentary on networking… you know, Face Book and the whole six degrees of separation thing. These two university professors did an experiment getting these people from all over the world to see if they could get a parcel to this dude in America through their network. It was unbelievable! A tribesman from Africa and an Arab from Egypt were successful among others, including an Australian. Guess how many hands the parcel went through to reach the target? Six.'

'Wow that is amazing.'

'Steve, I have a question for you.'

'Right what is it?'

'How would you feel if Andy moved in?'

'I don't have a problem. There's plenty of room but I think you'd better check with Mum and Dad first.'

'Oh sure, I fully intended to but I wanted to make sure you were comfortable with the idea of Andy and me living together.'

'Hold on, do you mean really living together, as partners?'

'Steve, I'm gay.'

'No, you can't be… you've had girlfriends. I've met a few.'

'I'm gay. The girls were just a smoke screen.'

'Well, I'll be fucked. Not in the Biblical sense. Rob, you're going to have to give me some time to think this through. It's a shock, I've got to admit.'

'I understand, mate, and if you're not happy about Andy moving in, it won't happen.'

'I certainly don't want to cause a problem between you two, Steve, but I can tell you, I love your brother very much.' Andy said with conviction.

Rob and Andy left the house intending to have dinner in an Indian restaurant in Carlton. On the way they changed their plans and decided to visit friends in St Kilda and discuss what had just happened and get some advice.

Steve sat there on the couch mulling over what he had just learnt about his big brother; he brother who was respected by all. The brother with the Mensa intellect, the brother who was gay! Not that there was anything wrong with that.

He came to the conclusion that Rob was his brother and he loved him as such. Who cares if he was gay?

Steve called Rob on his mobile and gave him his answer: Andy was welcome.

The next weekend Andy moved in and to Steve's surprise, the three of them got on famously.

The years passed and both brothers achieved excellent results. As it turned out, they both graduated in the same year, Rob with his Ph.D Medical Research and Steve with his Medical degree.

Rob had accepted a place at The Dementia Research Centre (DRC) in Sydney early in his studies and was still keen to take up the position. That would leave Steve in the house alone.

It was in the dead of winter, July, the three were sitting in front of the open fire in the living room, sipping scotch and discussing Rob and Andy's move to Sydney, when the telephone rang. Steve answered the phone to their father.

'Hello, mate, it's Dad. How's things at your end?'

'Good, Dad. How about you and Mum?'

'Is Rob with you?'

'Hi, Dad, I'm here!' Rob yelled out.

'Can you put the phone on loud speaker? I want to discuss something with you both.'

Andy sensed that he should leave the room.

'OK, Dad, it's on speaker. What's up?' said Steve.

'Both Mum and I visited a doctor this week.'

Both brothers got cold chill down their spines. 'Oh no, it's cancer,' they thought.

'Yeah, why?'

'We didn't want to alarm you until we had a definite diagnosis. Mum's been diagnosed with Early Onset Alzheimer's.'

'Oh my God!' they both shouted.

'How in the hell? I don't believe this. She's only fifty-five,' cried Rob.

'I have suspected something was wrong for a few months now but it seems to be getting worse. Her diagnosis identifies her at stage three, which means your mother is in the early stage.'

'What's been happening, Dad? What's stage three?' inquired Steve.

'She has a real problem identifying objects. She might call the coffee machine the blender etc. She also has been having trouble communicating in my work's social events or any other social events for that matter.'

'Anything else?'

'She will read an article in a newspaper magazine and immediately forget what she has just read. Overall it's not too bad but there's one thing for certain, she will progressively get worse until she reaches the final stage. You both know she has been playing Mah-jong every week with her girlfriends? Well now she has trouble remembering how to play. The strange thing is she might win one week and have trouble the following week.'

'This is terrible. Poor Mum.'

'So what are you going to do?' asked Rob.

'I've decided to resign and look after her full time until such a time as when she needs to go into a home. That could be a number of years or a lot sooner. There's really no way of knowing, as each person progresses differently.'

'So what happens in stage four and how many stages are there?' asked Steve.

'Stage four is titled "moderate cognitive decline". She will become more forgetful and her ability to perform mental arithmetic will decline. They tell me she will lose the memory of her life. She won't remember the law practice or if she does, it will be blurred. She will probably forget her girlhood days. Stage five is titled "moderately severe cognitive decline."

This stage is quite serious. She'll become confused as to where she is and what day it is. I'll probably have to help her choose her clothing to ensure she isn't dressed for a cold winter's day when it is actually thirty-five degrees outside and sweltering.

Stage six is called "severe cognitive decline". She will pretty much rely on me for all functions including going to the toilet. They've warned me that at this stage her personality might change. She should still be able to remember her name but not mine or yours for that matter. She should be able to recognise you, which is one consolation.

Apparently it's at this stage that they start to wander off and get lost. I'm going to keep a close watch on her. You can imagine what stage seven is.'

'You know we'll both support you both as much as we can, Dad,' said Rob with a tear in his eye.

'That's for sure. Anything we can do to help,' agreed Steve.

'Thank God I'm moving to Sydney. At least I'm close,' said Rob.

'Yes, mate, I'm sure you'll be a great support.'

'OK, boys, sorry to be the bearer of bad news. I'll call you soon.'

'Bye, Dad.'

Both brothers sat in silence for some time, lost in their own thoughts.

'As I said to Dad, thank Christ I'm moving up to Sydney. I can't do much but he'll need all the support he can get.'

'It's frustrating for me unless I can get an internship in Sydney but I don't like my chances.'

Steve was correct. All the Sydney internships were reserved for Sydney graduates. He would have to serve his time at St Vincent's and then move to Sydney.

On January 5, Rob was driven to the airport by his younger brother. Andy had not yet secured a position as a chemist in Sydney and therefore stayed in Melbourne still living in the Toorak house with Steve.

Both Steve and Andy gave Rob a hug and watched him disappear through the security gate.

Steve reflected on how much his family's lives had changed in the past six months.

Steak & Kidney Sydney

Chapter 5

Rob arrived in Sydney on Tuesday, August 25th. His father picked him up at the airport and drove him to the Kirribilli apartment where Bev, his mother, was waiting in the company of a good friend.

'How's Mum going, Dad?'

'No real change. You may find her pretty normal when we get home or she may be totally confused.'

'What does she do during the day to keep herself occupied? I mean she was such an active woman with her legal practice and such.'

'I take her out most days. She doesn't really mind whether it's a drive to the northern beaches or going to the hardware store. I gave up taking her to the movies as she just gets confused.'

'It must be pretty boring for you, Dad.'

'It's not about me, Rob, it's all about her. If I can make life a little more pleasant for her then I'll do anything I can to make it happen.'

'I know you will, Dad, I just thought being top of your game in the business world… well you know what I mean.'

'I do, but you do what you've got do. That's it.'

The Jaguar pulled into the underground parking station. John helped Rob with his luggage and placed it in his room.

Bev was on the balcony overlooking the harbour, drinking a cup of tea with her good friend, Julie. She looked up and saw her son.

'Robbie, darling, what are you doing here?'

'I've come for a visit, Mum, to see you and Dad.'

'Well that's wonderful where are you staying, darling?'

'Well, I thought you might put me up for a while.'

'John, is that all right? Do we have room?'

'Yes, darling, we have room. Why don't we have a drink? I think the sun is over the yardarm and we can have a chat. It's been a while since it was just the three of us.' Julie said her good byes.

Bev went to bed at about nine, leaving John and Rob to talk in private.

'So, Rob, did you notice a difference?'

'Oh sure, it's not the Mum I've always known in some respects but it's still Mum. She's still as attractive as ever and she can still hold a conversation. It throws you a bit when in the middle of talking she asks 'do you like my rings?' but overall, not too much different.'

'Yeah, she can appear to be quite normal but this morning she put on three bras.'

'What do you tell her?'

'You just have to act normally and suggest she would be more comfortable with just the one.'

'I can tell you, Dad, I'm going to put all my efforts to find a cure for this horrible bloody disease.'

'When do you start?'

'Tomorrow.'

'No mucking around then?'

'No, can hardly wait.'

'Well, Rob, I better let you go off to bed and get a good night's sleep. You better be bright- eyed and bushy- tailed as the saying goes.'

'Goodnight.'

The two men rose and gave each other a strong hug. They both retired to their respective bedrooms.

Rob had a fitful sleep; he couldn't stop thinking about his mother and the first day on the new job. A strange bed didn't help either.

He made himself breakfast the next morning, nothing too elaborate, just cornflakes and toast with vegemite. He didn't normally have coffee in the morning but decided he needed the caffeine to give him a boost.

'Good morning, Rob, how did you sleep?'

'Not too good, Dad, but you get that sometimes.'

'I hope it wasn't the bed? It's supposed to be a good one.'

'No, the bed was fine. Just a lot going on in my head.'

'Understand. Have you decided how you're getting to the lab?'

'I think I'll catch the ferry to Circular Quay. Apparently it's only a fifteen minute walk from there.'

'Good idea. The ferry wharf is only five minutes from here.'

'Well I better get my skates on, Dad! Wish me well.'

'You'll be fine, Rob. I'm looking to sharing a drink with you when you get home.'

'By the way, what are you and Mum doing today?'

'Haven't mapped it out yet but I'll think of something.'

Rob left the apartment and walked down the steep tree-lined street to catch the ferry, arriving just in time to board "The Lady Macquarie".

'I'd better leave five minutes earlier tomorrow,' he thought.

It was a beautiful morning and the harbour looked her best with the ferries and sail boats crossing the blue water just like the postcards you see in the tourist shops. They passed the Opera House, which was glistening in the morning sun. At school, back in Melbourne, they used to say the Opera House looked like copulating dinghies. He thought that might have been a bit of capital city rivalry.

32

Circular Quay was a mass of people, some disembarking while others were boarding. He made it through and began his walk to the offices of DRC.

Approaching the receptionist desk, he introduced himself and requested Dr Julian Wang be informed of his presence.

The receptionist, Zoë, was aware of his imminent arrival and made quite a fuss. He sat in the reception area and she brought him a cup of coffee – another one.

He only had to wait ten minutes when Dr Wang greeted him and asked Rob to follow him to his office.

'Take a seat Robert. Can I get my secretary to get you a coffee?'

'No thanks, Dr Wang. I'm fine thank you.'

'OK, now let's go over a few ground rules. My name is Julian not Dr Wang.'

'Right, well my name is Rob not Robert.'

'Excellent now we've got that sorted out.'

'We have been looking forward to you starting here. We have heard excellent things about you from Dr Wilson at Melbourne University.'

'Well I hope I live up to your expectations, Julian.'

'I am sure you will. Now I understand your grandmother died from Alzheimer's?'

'I'm afraid so.'

'Was this your motivating force to take up the study of dementia?'

'Initially, yes.'

'Initially?'

'My mother has been diagnosed with stage three Alzheimer's also.'

'Oh, I am sorry to hear that, Rob.'

'Yeah, my father has quit his job as CEO at Pfizer to care for her full time. So as you can imagine, Jason, I am motivated to help you find a cure.'

'I should bring you up to date with what we are doing at DRC.

The Dementia Research Centre (DRC) was established to facilitate the testing of new drugs for the treatment of Alzheimer's disease, particularly drugs that might not otherwise be tested by industry. We cooperate with more than seventy research sites in Australia, Britain, United States and Canada. DRC investigates promising interventions.

Our clinical trials focus on interventions that may benefit people across the disease spectrum, from the detection of Alzheimer's-related brain changes in people free of symptoms to the treatment of agitation in people with Alzheimer's dementia. This includes the testing of:

Drugs that lack patent protection

Drugs under patent protection that are already marketed for other uses but which might prove useful for treating people with Alzheimer's disease

Novel compounds developed by individuals, academia, and pharmaceutical and small biotech companies

In addition to testing new therapies, the DRC develops new evaluation instruments for clinical trials and innovative approaches to Alzheimer's disease, clinical trial design and analysis. The DRC emphasizes collaboration and data sharing among its partner sites and with other research institutions.

We are one of the few clinics that use animals in clinical tests.

DRC is seeding drug development and increasing the number of promising therapies tested in people at the earliest stages of the disease, when treatment may be most effective. To date, the DRC has conducted thirty studies. It also provides infrastructure support to other Government funded clinical efforts, such as the Alzheimer's Disease Neuro Imaging Initiative.

'Do you have any questions Rob?'

'No, not at this stage thanks Julian.'

'Well I think it's time to show you the Lab and where you will be working.'

The two research scientists made their way to the laboratory where Dr Wang introduced Rob to the people he would be working with. Rob was impressed with the sophistication of the equipment and the friendliness of the staff.

Rob completed his first day with a feeling of satisfaction. He was sure he had chosen the right institution to develop his career and help find a cure for dementia.

Laboratory Rats

Chapter 6

When Rob walked into his parents' apartment both of them were on the balcony with a wine in hand.

'Hello, you two, couldn't wait for me I see.'

'Hi, Rob. We didn't know what time you would get home. Grab a glass and join us,' said his father.

Rob went to the kitchen and selected a large wine glass from the cabinet and returned to the balcony to join his parents. John poured him a glass of German Riesling.

'Well, Rob, don't keep us in suspense. How did it go?' asked his father.

'Great, I'm convinced I made the right choice.'

'Well, we can only hope you feel that way in twelve months.'

'What do you mean by that?'

'It's only your first day, Rob, you haven't even sat at your workstation. From my experience, first impressions are pretty accurate but you never know.'

'Well thanks for all the positive vibes, Dad.'

'I'm sure it's the beginning of a fantastic career, mate. I'm just saying it doesn't always work out. Just be realistic in your expectations.'

'I know what you're saying but having inspected the lab and meeting the people, I can't imagine it wouldn't work out.'

'That's great, Rob, we're both happy for you. Aren't we Bev?'

'We are, very happy.'

'How did you go on the ferry?'

'Good, no problem. What a wonderful way to get to work but it might be a bit different in a thunderstorm or a large swell.'

'Your mother and I thought it would be nice for us all to go out for dinner and celebrate your first day of what we are sure will be a brilliant career. What do you think?'

'Sounds great. Where are we going?'

'In Restaurant' which is an excellent seafood place at Neutral Bay.'

'OK, sounds good. I'll just have a quick shower and be back in a tick.'

The three Iffingers caught a taxi to the restaurant and were seated by the waiter. John ordered a bottle of Tasmanian Sauvignon Blanc and they toasted Rob wishing him every success.

'Thanks, Mum and Dad, I appreciate your good wishes and the hospitality you have extended to me since I arrived in Sydney. I do have something to tell you, though; I will be moving out very soon when my partner arrives from Melbourne. I will make sure I'm near to you although I can't afford Kirribilli.'

'We didn't know you were in a serious relationship. What's her name?'

'Dad, Mum, it's not a 'her', it's a him.'

'What! You're kidding aren't you? Are you telling us you're gay?'

'That's exactly what I'm telling you. I think I've been gay all my life.'

'Well, who is he?'

'Andy, the guy who has been sharing with Steve and me in the Toorak house.'

'So Steve knows?'

'Yes of course, Dad. We shared a room.'

'Well I'm shocked but if that's the way it is…'

The remainder of the meal was eaten in virtual silence. Rob felt very uncomfortable but with Andy arriving in a couple of weeks, he felt he needed to inform his parents of their relationship.

The three of them said goodnight. His mother gave him a kiss and whispered in his ear 'I love you, darling.'

The next morning Rob went off to work having not sighted his Mother or Father at breakfast. He knew it would be tough for them initially but he also knew they would accept his sexuality.

He was right: it only took a couple of days for his relationship with both his parents to get back on an even keel.

Rob found a very nice apartment in Crows Nest, which was close to the train station and restaurants. Andy was due to fly in on the weekend so Rob went on a furniture-buying spree at Ikea.

The day came and Rob hired a car to pick up Andy. He figured he'd wait for Andy to help him choose the right car to buy.

'How was the flight, mate?'

'Pretty good. The coffee was crap and the muffins were dry but apart from that, it was OK.'

'Airline food has never been any good,' Rob agreed.

'So you've found us a new home?'

'Yeah. Nothing too fancy as we're both starting new jobs so it will do until we're on our feet and earning good money.'

'So what you're saying is, it's not up to the standard of the Toorak home.'

'No, not quite.'

Rob pulled into the car park of unit sixteen. He helped Andy lug his luggage up the two flights of stairs and into the unit.

'This isn't too bad, Rob, in fact it's quite nice. We've even got a view of the city… mind you, it's a bloody long way away.'

'Why don't you dump your bags and I'll shout you lunch at my favourite café around the corner?'

'Sounds like an excellent plan.'

The two lovers walked the kilometre to "Stone the Crow" chatting the whole way about Rob's new position and Andy's job at the large pharmacy at Chatswood, a prosperous shopping mall just a few kilometres from the unit.

Over lunch, Rob told Andy about divulging their relationship to his parents. He assured Andy that all would be well. He also brought him up to date with his mother's condition. Andy was very empathetic and assured Rob he was there for him.

'So, Rob, when do you think I should meet your oldies?'

'I think we should leave it for a couple of weeks. You know, let them get used to the idea that their son is a raving poofter.'

'Rob!'

'Just joking, mate.'

'Well when we tell your folks, I'll tell mine.'

'It's going to be a fun time. Maybe what we should do is take part in the Mardi Gras and they can see us on television.'

'Now there's an idea. We could be part of the "Professional Poofters" float.

'Bullshit, there's no such thing.'

'There is! All the gay lawyers and accountants, chemists and research scientists get together.'

'Now you're pushing it.'

'Yeah, just kidding.'

They finished their lunch and wandered back to the unit to get Andy unpacked and settled in.

My Brilliant Career
Chapter 7

Rob settled into his career as a research scientist at DRC, where he was in charge of a small group including:

Pathologist

Clinical Biochemist

Pathologist's Assistant

Biomedical Scientist

Medical Laboratory Technician

Medical Laboratory Assistant

Phlebotomist

They had all recently started at DRC after a large corporate donation was made by one of Australia's largest pharmaceutical companies.

The team working with Rob had no real knowledge of Alzheimer's disease and what caused it. They had all had been working on other research projects with various research Laboratories around Australia and internationally.

He decided to run a one-day seminar to bring them up to speed.

'OK, everybody; we are about to embark on an incredible journey of discovery. Our mandate is to find a cure for Alzheimer's disease. Dr Wang has already made good progress and it is up us to continue his important work.

Do any of you have a relative or friend with Alzheimer's?'

Three of the seven attendees held their hands up.

'That's about what I expected. This insidious disease has touched over forty per cent of this group, including me.'

'Named after German physician, Dr Alois Alzheimer, who first described the disease in 1906, Alzheimer's disease is a degenerative condition of the brain, characterised by loss of memory and cognitive function. Although there is currently no cure for Alzheimer's disease, it is our mission to discover one. Currently it can be managed and the symptoms alleviated for a time. A person may live from three to twenty years with Alzheimer's disease, the average being seven years.

You are all probably aware that Alzheimer's is the most common form of dementia, accounting for around half of all dementias. In 2009 the number of Australians with dementia was estimated to be 245,000. Due to our ageing population, the incidence of dementia is estimated to rise above 1.1 million by 2050. Every five years after the age of sixty-five, the likelihood of living with dementia doubles and the disease affects one in four people aged eighty-five and over. In 2004, the cost of Alzheimer's disease alone in Australia was estimated to be $3.6 billion.

There are two types of Alzheimer's disease, sporadic and familial (hereditary). In the sporadic form, the disease is usually diagnosed after the age of sixty-five and is by far the most common form. In the less common familial form, the disease runs in families and usually affects people in their forties to fifties.

My Grandmother contracted it at age sixty, my mother at the age of fifty-four.'

'Excuse me, Doctor, are you saying my chances for contracting Alzheimer's is high because my father has it?' asked Sophie, the Pathologist's Assistant.'

'No, not at all, Sophie, in fact there is very little chance you would contract it.'

'So what causes Alzheimer's disease?'

'Apart from familial or hereditary Alzheimer's disease, the cause of Alzheimer's is not currently known. A major risk factor is age, although the reasons for this are not well understood. A variety of suspects, including environmental factors, biochemical disturbances and immune processes are being investigated, although it is most likely to be a combination of factors that cause the disease. It is known, however, that head injury, particularly repeated trauma, increases the risk of developing Alzheimer's. Poor cardiovascular health and smoking have also been linked to the disease. A genetic mutation on the ApoE gene is implicated in Alzheimer's and this gene, along with several other genes, will be part of our investigation.

The symptoms of Alzheimer's disease are caused by the loss of nerve cells and pathways in the areas of the brain that are vital to memory and other mental abilities. Plaques, which contain misfolded proteins, called beta amyloid form in the brain many years before the clinical signs of Alzheimer's are obvious. Another protein called tau, abnormally aggregates in the brain cells causing them to die. It is not known if this pathology, which is used to definitively diagnose Alzheimer's disease after death, initiates the disease or results from the disease.

DRC is taking a range of approaches to investigate Alzheimer's disease. Some of our scientists are researching the mechanisms at the synapses (where one neuron makes a connection with another) that are important in memory formation and trying to understand if these mechanisms are somehow involved in contributing to neuronal death in Alzheimer's disease. In particular, we focus on signalling pathways regulating neuroplasticity, or the ability of the brain to change or 're-wire' itself. This process is uniquely advanced

42

in humans and defects can lead to neuro-degenerative disorders. We have mapped new pathways controlling neuroplasticity and are currently determining if they are dysregulated in the brains of Alzheimer's patients. The goal of this work is to identify novel therapeutic targets or biomarkers that can be used for early and specific detection of Alzheimer's disease.

Our research project involves the possibility of harnessing the brain's own adult stem cells, which normally function to repair injury to the brain and make new nerve cell connections, to help treat Alzheimer's disease and other neurodegenerative conditions. Dr Wang and his team have identified a molecule that is able to stimulate neurogenesis, which would underpin brain repair. This is important because it is believed that brain repair could provide part of a cure for neurodegenerative diseases. It is our mission to continue Dr Wang's research, we have an enormous amount of work to do to understand how this molecule acts to bring about this regeneration, determine if the molecule has any therapeutic potential, and identify other molecules that may be important for stimulating regeneration and stem cell therapies.'

The group left the lecture room full of hope and enthusiasm for the work they were about to undertake. They all felt they could really make a difference.

The following day the team began their research in earnest. The dynamics of the team seemed to work from day one.

Pathologist: Amy

Clinical Biochemist: Rosie

Pathologists' Assistant: Peter

Biomedical Scientist: Pierre

Medical Laboratory Technician: Tony

Medical Laboratory Assistant: Emma

Phlebotomist: Dianne

Rob was the leader and Medical Research Doctor. There was no way of knowing how long the project would last but there was some comfort in knowing their research was fully funded for a further five years.

Tragedy
Chapter 8

2012

It was Friday night and Dr Julian Wang was having drinks with his employees, a tradition at DRC since the lab was established. It gave everybody a chance to unwind and mix with the other research groups. Everybody was in good spirits as the various research projects were starting to show real promise.

At six o'clock Julian bade his staff farewell as he had an industry dinner to attend, not that he was particularly looking forward to the black tie event. There was no way he could give his apologies as he was to receive a lifetime achievement award.

He strolled down to the basement car park and pressed the key to unlock the BMW Seven series, his pride and joy.

He was only five minutes into the thirty minute drive home when a Holden V8 went through a red light hitting the BMW at what the police estimated was ninety kilometres an hour. Julian's car was hit on the driver's door crushing him between the two cars; he was killed instantly.

The police were on the scene within fifteen minutes and the recalcitrant driver who had survived with minor injuries was breath tested and returned a reading of 0.331, almost seven times the legal limit.

He was arrested and taken to the police station for questioning.

Julian Wang had a wife of thirty years, Alison, and two children, Michael, aged twenty-five and Bianca, aged thirty.

His funeral was held on the following Friday at St Andrew's Cathedral in central Sydney. Over five hundred people attended, including the NSW Premier, the Governor General and the Federal Minister for Health.

It was a very sad occasion; an act of total stupidity took a wonderful and dedicated research scientist.

Rob and the rest of the staff were absolutely devastated. He had been working with Julian for the past four years and held him in the highest esteem.

He knew he had to complete the research that Julian had instigated. They had made significant gains and were very close to a cure.

He and Andy were enjoying living in Sydney and they had recently purchased a two-bedroom apartment at McMahon's Point overlooking the harbour and the city.

Andy was now the senior Chemist at Chatswood; he had six chemists and twenty counter staff reporting to him.

They had bought an Alfa Romeo Spider and enjoyed nothing more than driving around the North Shore with the top down on a sunny day.

Apart from Julian's premature death, life had been very good for both of them.

It was a Thursday when Rob's mobile phone rang.

'Hi Rob, it's Andy.'

'Hi mate, what's up?'

'Can I ask you a favour? I just used the last of the coffee beans. Can you drop into Mario's and pick up a kilo on your way home please?'

'Are you home, mate?'

'Yeah,I told you this morning I had the afternoon off. Don't you remember?'

'Oh sorry, mate, yes of course I remember. OK I'll grab a bag. Anything else we need?'

'No just the beans.'

'Right then see you about six. Have a red waiting for me.'

'Done.'

Rob walked in the door looking forward to relaxing with Andy. It had been a tough day at the lab.

'I'm home, darling,' Rob said in jest.

46

'Hi, how are you?'

'Stuffed, looking forward to a wine.'

'Done, it's already poured did you pick up the coffee beans?'

'Oh shit, I forgot. Sorry mate.'

'I can't believe you forgot! Fucking hell.'

'I'm sorry, it's not the end of the world.'

'Yeah, I suppose not, but you are becoming very forgetful lately. Are you OK?'

'To tell you the truth, I'm starting to become a bit worried. I'm also forgetting stuff at work.'

'With your family history, maybe you should get assessed.'

'Don't say that, for God's sake.'

'Well you, more than most, know it can happen even at your age.'

The two men enjoyed their wine on the balcony and didn't discuss memory again. Well, not as it related to Rob. They did discuss Bev, Rob's mother.

'I heard from Dad today.'

'Right, how's it all going?'

'Not good. As you know, Mum was in the fourth stage of Alzheimer's. Well, she had another assessment and they've reclassified her as fifth stage, verging on sixth.'

'Shit, what does that mean for them?'

'It means she will have to go into a nursing home in the near future.'

'Oh no, that's sad. What's your Dad going to do?'

'He thinks that the best facility is in the Blue Mountains.'

'What's it called?'

47

'Ah, it's called… fuck, I can't remember. This is ridiculous! Hold on, Blue something… Blue Mountains. No that's not it. Blue Hills… no.'

'Don't worry, mate, it will come to you. No big deal.'

The two of them sat down to a Rogan Josh curry Andy had cooked that afternoon.

They were in the middle of a conversation relating to the trip to Europe they were planning when Rob stopped and blurted out.

'It's Blue Haven Nursing Home, in Leura. That's it.'

'So it's a big drive for John every day.'

'He is considering selling the Kirribilli apartment and buying a place up there.'

'Well anyway, it's bloody sad.'

'Yeah, but we always knew it would come to this. It's inevitable.'

'This won't affect our trip to France, will it?'

'No, life has to go on.'

'Is Steve going to be able to stay in the apartment while we are away?'

'Oh yeah, I forgot to tell you he has secured a position in the emergency ward at RPA. He starts on September 1 but will arrive in Sydney in August.'

'That's great. It will be great for your Mum and Dad too.'

'Yeah, Dad's really looking forward to it. He's been hanging out for him to move up here for a couple of years. Steve just couldn't find the right position.'

'So he'll be here a couple of weeks before we leave?'

'Yep, no problems.'

'Do you want to talk about the trip now or would you rather leave it for another night?'

'I'm fine. Have you found somewhere in Sarlat yet?'

'Yeah I have. You're going to love it, it's an old sandstone villa right in the middle of the village, fully restored.'

'Great, so we can just walk down to the restaurants and shops and stagger our way back home.'

'That's the general idea.'

'How long are we in Sarlat for?'

'Well, we had agreed for one week but I can change it if you like.'

'No no, that's fine, perfect in fact. Where are we going after that again?'

'We're heading up to the Loire Valley to take in some magnificent châteaux.'

'That's right. I can hardly wait. I've always wanted to see Château of Sully-sur-Loire and Château of Chambord not to mention Royal Château of Amboise and Chenonceau Château. My Mum gave me a coffee table book of all the great châteaux in the Loire Valley and I've wanted to visit them ever since. That must have been when I was about fifteen.'

'So just to recap our itinerary, we fly into Paris on the 16th September, we spend four nights in Paris staying in a beautiful little hotel, Le Marais. It's walking distance to the Louvre and Musée d'Orsay as well as Notre Dame. Needless to say, the shopping and the eating will be magnificent.

We then pick up our Golf and drive down to Versailles. You're not going to believe the opulence. No wonder the French had a revolution.

Then it's off to Amboise in the middle of the Loire Valley. We're staying at Le Manoir Les Minimes, a beautiful old hotel, for two nights. We're going to need it to visit all the châteaux you have on your list.'

'Is two days long enough Andy? I see this as the highlight of the trip.'

'I think so. Believe me, you will be châteauxed out by the time we finish.'

'OK, you're the much travelled one, I'll take your word for it.'

'From the valley, we drive to Bordeaux, a place I'm sure you will enjoy, all the red wine you can drink. We're staying at another beautiful elegant hotel, Les Sources de Caudalie.'

We're there for two days then we drive to Sarlat.

After Sarlat and the Dordogne we drive to Nice where we can pretend to be rich and famous. We're in Nice for two days then we fly to Venice.'

'This is fantastic, mate, all these places I've dreamed of since I was a kid.'

'In Venice we're staying at Hotel Ai Reali, right on a canal so we'll be able to hail a gondola from the front steps. We stay in Venice for four days and then we jump on the Flying Kangaroo and fly home.

So, what do you think?'

'I think it all sounds great. I'm just thankful you're with me to lead the way.'

'Come on, it's time for bed.'

'I'm with you. I'm stuffed.'

'That's a shame.'

'Not that stuffed.'

Dr Iffinger, I Presume
Chapter 9

Steve finally finished his medical degree at Melbourne Uni, it had been a tough five years in relation to the workload but he dedicated himself to the course and passed with distinctions. He had continued with his involvement in the Foot Lights Club and had been told by other students that if he ever decided to leave medicine he could become a professional actor. His initial reason for joining was to meet girls and he had achieved that aim well and truly. He had the reputation of being a real ladies' man.

He rang his Mum and Dad weekly and his brother, Rob, every other week. It had been difficult being in Melbourne when the rest of the family lived in Sydney. He flew up a couple of times a year predominantly to see his Mother. Over the few years since diagnosis, he could see the deterioration in her condition well; everybody could.

Steve had taken up surfing on the basis that one of his girlfriends was a "hot surfer" and it gave him the excuse of going away with her every weekend down to Torquay and the beaches along the "Great Ocean Road" including the famous "Bells Beach".

When the relationship broke up, Steve continued on; he was hooked on the sport and the lifestyle. He bought a Volkswagen Kombi Van, which was decked out as a camper.

He would finish lectures on a Friday, generally around two in the afternoon and head down to Torquay for a surf before heading for the pub.

He had been applying for positions at various Sydney hospitals but there seemed plenty of Sydney Uni graduates to fill the available jobs.

If it weren't for the fact that his family now resided in Sydney he would have been quite happy working at St Vincent's and living in the family home in Toorak.

Working in the emergency department gave Steve a taste of pretty much every conceivable injury and its treatment, including some wild and wonderful cases which were usually discussed later in the hospital canteen.

One example was where a neighbour of a newly-wed couple was worried when she didn't hear her rather noisy neighbours for a while. A few days later, she peered through their letterbox and through the windows. But there was no sign of anyone. Concerned for the young couple, she called the police. The officers promptly broke down the door, and searched the house. They found the young woman gagged and tied to the bed, naked. Her husband was lying on the floor with two broken legs, wearing a Superman outfit. They later explained that they had been engaged in a superhero role-playing fantasy, and the costumed husband had broken his legs attempting to jump onto his wife from atop the dresser. Of course, the woman was unable to help him!

Both were brought into the emergency ward, she, suffering from dehydration and he, still in his Superman outfit.

Another case, which caused lots of laughter amongst the medical staff, was where an unconscious thirty-year-old man was brought into Emergency. His girlfriend had found him lying naked on the floor of his bathroom and called an ambulance. He was found to have a large lump on the top of his head and strangely, several scratches on his scrotum. Steve decided the lump was possibly caused by a fall or a knock to the head. However the source of the scratches remained a mystery until he woke up and provided Steve with the following explanation. He said he had been cleaning his bathtub while naked having just stepped out of the shower. He had been kneeling on the floor beside the tub when his cat, apparently transfixed by the rhythmic swaying of his scrotum, lunged forward, sinking its claws into this pendulous target. This caused the man to rocket upward, striking his head on the top frame of the shower door.

Steve enjoyed recounting this story to his colleagues in the canteen.

Steve completed his intern year at St Vincent's hospital and was offered a permanent position to join the medical staff. He accepted and continued at the hospital until a position was offered at RPS in Sydney three years later. He knew he was obligated to accept, despite loving his job at St Vincent's and enjoying living in Melbourne, his hometown. Taking the role at RPA in Sydney would allow him to be near his family and support his parents.

He took a four-week break between jobs and flew to Indonesia where he surfed at Mentawai Island, Panaitan Island and Bali. It was just what the doctor ordered and he returned to Melbourne, invigorated, ready to take up the new position.

Steve had a few things to organise before the move; he'd assured his father that he would find suitable tenants for the house and a storage facility to store the furniture. His father had transferred the wine collection to Sydney a few years before.

The Estate Agent found tenants, a married couple, both doctors, so that was one thing out of the way. He also arranged for the furniture to be transported to a very reputable storage facility. Steve wondered why his father kept the furniture when he didn't need it; he seemed to think his father still wanted a connection to Melbourne.

On 15th August Steve boarded a plane to Sydney and a new life. He thought it would be only for a few years until his Mum passed on, then he would return to his much loved Melbourne.

Rob and Andy picked him up from the airport and began driving him home to their McMahon's Point unit.

     'Bloody hell, mate, I think Sydney has more bloody traffic than Melbourne.'

     'Yeah, it's pretty intense. Still, there's no use complaining; we're stuck with it.'

     'I'm hoping I can use public transport. If I get a place on the rail line, I'll be able to catch a train.'

     'You should be able to. Anywhere from North Sydney to Artarmon would suit you.'

     Finally they arrived at the unit, where both Andy and Rob helped Steve with his luggage including his surfboard.

'Wow, guys, this place is fantastic! Take a look at the view! I'm going to enjoy living here when you go away.'

'No wild parties, OK?'

'As if! I don't know anyone in Sydney anyway.'

'Just kidding, mate.'

'Well, it's five o'clock, drink time,' announced Andy.

'What's your poison, Steve? Do you still drink Scotch?'

'Is the Pope a Catholic?'

'What about you, Rob?'

'Yeah, I think I might have a Scotch as well, thanks Andy.'

'Three Scotches it is then. On the rocks?'

'Is there any other way?' laughed Steve.

The three men sat out on the balcony sipping their J&B and taking in the view. There was a big cruise liner sailing under the harbour bridge and the small racing yachts were darting all around it.

'So, how's Mum going? I speak to them on the phone and Skype but it's difficult to know how they really are.'

'The Alzheimer's is progressing; there's no doubt about that. She hasn't used my name for over a year now but she still recognises me. She doesn't really understand who Andy is and why we are always together when we visit her but that's to be expected.'

'So does she understand what's going on about her?'

'Not really. She gets confused easily. Dad told me she tried to flush her bra down the toilet the other day.'

'Bloody hell.'

'I don't think it is too long before she goes into a nursing home. Dad has already put her application in to a home in the Blue Mountains.'

'That's sad, but realistic. He will get some respite at last.'

'He's planning on moving up there so he can visit every day.'

'That's dedication.'

'Well, he has been married to her for thirty-five years. He loves her now just as much as he did when he married her.'

'I hope I eventually find a partner that loves me after thirty five years.'

'We're going over to their apartment tomorrow night for dinner. I promised Dad that Andy and I would cook Coq au vin .'

'Good one. So they have accepted Andy into the family, as it were?'

'Oh yeah, Andy and Dad are great mates and he is wonderful with Mum.'

Andy returned to the balcony with a large plate of nachos, which they all got stuck into.

The Eyes are the Window to the Soul

Chapter 10

Rob was becoming concerned with his own memory loss. Not only was he forgetting grocery items and such at home, he was forgetting critical things in his work at the lab.

He decided to approach his second-in-charge, Dr Henry Lee, a brilliant doctor who had migrated from China ten years prior.

'Henry, can I ask you to join me for a coffee at Aromas? I need to talk to you away from the lab.'

'Sure, Rob. Nothing wrong I hope?'

'No just a private chat.'

The two friends and colleagues walked the kilometre to their favourite coffee spot.

'Henry, I'm getting very concerned that I may be contracting familial Alzheimer's disease.'

'Are you sure, Rob?'

'No I'm not sure, mate. That's where you come in.'

'I don't follow you.'

'I want you to conduct the eye test on me.'

'You know that it is in the experimental stage, mate. It has worked with mice but very few human experiments have taken place.'

'I don't see it as a big deal! It's just a fucking eye test, for God's sake.'

'OK, OK, I'll do it. When do you want me to arrange it?'

'This afternoon when we get back to the lab. I need to know before Andy and I go on our trip.'

'You know it may not be conclusive; we will have to do some more tests if the eye examination shows a positive result.'

'I understand.'

The two doctors returned to the lab and Henry prepared the equipment. He drew the curtains so none of the other workers would see it was Rob being tested.

Rob knew that diagnosing Alzheimer's disease could be a long and complicated process; after all, he had dedicated his professional life to the identification and cure of this debilitating disease. He was not keen to undertake a CT scan or a spinal tap. His logic for the retina scan was to keep his concerns secret for the time being.

In studies undertaken in the DRC lab, it had been discovered that the thickness of a particular layer of retinal cells might serve as an indication of Alzheimer's progression.

Henry was looking for biomarkers for early disease detection. It was DRC's objective to prevent Alzheimer's… and to test new drugs

DRC were hoping to incorporate this as a new biomarker for drug trials and potentially for screening and prognosis.

Currently, there are two leading biomarkers that physicians can utilize to diagnose Alzheimer's. One is the build-up of beta-amyloid plaques in the brain, which can be observed through positron emission tomography (PET) or computed tomography (CT) scans. The other involves measuring changes in protein levels of the cerebrospinal fluid – the liquid surrounding the brain and spinal cord.

Hoping to find a simpler biomarker, Henry and his team decided to analyse the relationship between the eyes and dementia. According to Henry, the retina serves as a direct extension of a person's brain.

'The retinas have neurons themselves that send projections straight into the brain,' Henry maintained.

'Those nerve cells are directly connected to the brain via the optic nerve. So when looking at the retina, it gives a window to see the brain and its neurons.'

The DCR Laboratory analysed a group of mice that had been genetically engineered to develop Alzheimer's disease, observing the thicknesses of the six layers in their retinas. They found that there was significant loss in thickness to both the inner nuclear layer, which experienced an average thirty seven per cent loss of neurons, and the retinal ganglion cell layer, which experienced an average forty nine per cent loss.

According to Henry, these two retinal layers may be most vulnerable to neuron loss because they are larger than the other layers.

Henry's test on Rob was an optical coherence tomography (OCT).

Rob sat down in the optometrists chair while Henry conducted the OCT.

Once completed, Henry asked Rob to return to his office while he analysed the results.

About forty minutes later Henry knocked on Rob's office door.

'Come in, mate and close the door behind you.'

'Well, Rob, I've got your results and they're pretty conclusive.'

'Pretty conclusive of what?'

'I'm sorry, mate, you tested positive to Alzheimer's.'

'Fuck it!'

'I don't know how progressed you are but my guess would be stage two.'

'Judging on the memory loss I've been suffering, I think you're probably right. Shit!'

'What are you going to do?'

'I'm going to Europe with Andy, that's what I'm going to do. After that, fucked if I know.'

'Mate, we are so close to a cure, as you know, and a large part of the success goes down to you. We may be able to arrest it.'

'You mean use me as a guinea pig?'

'It's been proven on the mice so we push the human experiments a little forward. Nobody needs to know, just you and me.'

'Let me think about it for a little while, Henry. I appreciate what you're trying to do.'

Rob caught the ferry across the harbour and then a taxi home. He didn't remember the journey as he was lost in his own thoughts.

'How could this happen to me? I've dedicated myself to finding a cure for Alzheimer's and the bastard has come back to bite me. It hardly seems fair.

It's following the Iffingers from generation to generation. I'm glad I'll never be a dad.'

He arrived at the apartment and greeted Andy in the usual way.

'Mate, I'm cooking you dinner tonight.'

'Sorry, Rob, I've already prepared it, we're having John Dory pan-fried with chips and salad. A good old Aussie fish and chips.'

'OK, you've talked me into it. Come on, let's have a drink.'

'Sure, would you like a wine?'

59

'No, I think I'll have a malt whiskey. The Larks is what I fancy.'

'Oh I see. Getting into the top shelf. Have you had a win today?'

'Not really. I'll tell you over our drink.'

The two men sat down and for a while admired the view and the activity on the harbour.

'Andy, I got some news today which I wasn't thrilled about.'

'What, mate?'

'I've been diagnosed as stage two Alzheimer's.'

'Bullshit, no way! You can't be.'

'I took a test, a new type which examines the retina. The results came back positive.

You know my memory has been getting worse. It started to really worry me, so I asked Henry to conduct the test. He's the only person at DRC who knows.'

'What are you going to do?'

'I have an opportunity to trial a new treatment that we have tested on mice. It reverses the disease and cures it completely.'

'Well, fucking trial it.'

'It's not that simple. I would be the first human to try it. Because it works on mice doesn't necessarily mean it will work on me.'

'It's got to be worth a punt, surely. Are there any possible side effects?'

'I don't know... a few.'

'Well, I still think it's got to be worth a try.'

'Henry offered to run the trial clandestinely. You would be the only other person aware of what is going on.'

'You're not going to tell your Father?'

'No, not at this stage. I would rather tell him when it's over and I've beaten the bloody thing.'

'Fair enough. So can you explain how it works, this miracle cure?'

'I, and my research team's objective over the past few years has been to develop a pill which would cure Alzheimer's

The compound we have discovered works by blocking a faulty signal in brains affected by neurodegenerative diseases, which shuts down the production of essential proteins, leading to brain cells being unprotected and dying off.

As you're aware, we have tested it on mice with prion disease - the best animal model of human neurodegenerative disorders. We are fairly confident the same principles would apply in a human brain with debilitating brain diseases such as Alzheimer's or Parkinson's.

We believe it's the first time a substance has been given to mice that prevents brain disease. The exciting thing is, the drug is given orally like any other pill.

However my program will be a course of injections to ensure confidentiality.

In debilitating brain diseases like Alzheimer's, the production of new proteins in the brain is shut down by a build-up of "misfolded proteins" or amyloids. This build-up leads to an "over-activation" of a natural defence mechanism that stops essential proteins being produced. Without these proteins to protect them, brain cells die off - leading to the symptoms of diseases like Alzheimer's.

The compound we discovered works by inhibiting an enzyme, known as PERK, which plays a key role in activating this defence mechanism. In mice with prion's disease, it restored proteins to protect brain cells "stopping the disease in its tracks", restoring some normal behaviours and preventing memory loss.

You asked me if there were any side effects? The answer is probably yes, it certainly was the case in the mice, including weight loss and mild diabetes, which was caused by damage to the pancreas.

What's encouraging is a drug in the form of a pill stops the progressive death of neurons in the brain as found, for instance, in Alzheimer's disease. I admit, Andy, this study has been done in mice, not man; and it is prion disease, not Alzheimer's that has been cured. However, there is considerable evidence that the way neurons die in both diseases is similar; and lessons learned in mice from prion disease have proved accurate guides to attenuate the progress of Alzheimer's disease in patients.

Andy what you need to understand is this drug has never been used on a human with Alzheimer's; however, from the test results there's convincing evidence that it can arrest neuro-degeneration caused by amyloid in the brain.

So, here endeth the lesson.'

'So, when do you start the treatment?'

'I take it you fully understand the risks and possible implications?'

'I trust you, mate. You're my soul mate and I don't want to lose you. If it takes a calculated risk to cure you, so be it.'

'OK, well I thought we should continue on the grand tour and begin soon after we return.'

'Are you sure you don't want to start treatment straight away? I have no problem delaying the trip.'

'No, I want to go; four or five weeks will make no difference to my condition.'

'Right, well let's have our fish and chips, shall we?'

The Grand Tour

Chapter 11

The day arrived when Steve and Andy were to depart for the grand tour of Europe; Steve drove them out to the airport. Steve, like his father, had no idea Rob had been diagnosed with Alzheimer's. They said their goodbyes with a hug and the two intrepid travellers disappeared into the terminal. It was the usual scene inside with people scrambling everywhere and more queues than a billiard player's tournament.

They looked up to the huge flight information board and found their flight, QF541 to Paris. The usual delays through security occurred but they passed through eventually.

Before making their way to the departure lounge they visited the duty free stores. Both purchased a litre of spirit; Rob bought a bottle of eighteen-year-old MacCallum's Malt and Andy, a bottle of Gordon's Gin.

They bought some magazines and headed for the lounge.

They had been waiting in the lounge for forty-five minutes when the announcement to board was made. They were stopping over in Dubai to break up the trip however the flight was nearly sixteen hours. They both thanked God they decided to pay the extra and fly business class.

On arrival they were picked up by the Atlantis's limousine and driven to the sixteen hundred-room luxury hotel situated on The Palm, an artificial sand island shaped like a palm tree. Their room had a view of the enormous aquarium surrounding the hotel; they lay on the bed watching manta rays swimming past.

It seemed like a bit of a waste as they were both exhausted; they ordered room service and went to bed. Next morning their plane departed at ten am, which meant they had to check out by seven.

They boarded the plane and settled into their business class seats knowing they only had a seven-hour flight in front of them.

Paris

Andy had been to Paris before but it was Rob's first trip. As they neared central Paris, Rob was in awe.

'I just caught a glimpse of the Eiffel Tower... it's amazing.'

'We'll climb to the top while we're here, mate. The view is truly fantastic.'

Let's go out this afternoon. I know we're both buggered from the flight but I just can't wait to see it.'

'How's this for an idea? Seeing we're already in a taxi, why don't I ask the driver to conduct a little tour? It will help you get your bearings when we're out and about tomorrow and will satisfy your urge to see Paris for now, anyway.'

'Great idea.'

Andy told the taxi driver in his best schoolboy French the route they wished to go. He didn't have a problem: the fare would be increased by quite a margin.

The first port of call was the Eiffel Tower, where Rob insisted on stopping so he could take a photo despite the fact they would be returning the next day. He was like a kid on his first overseas trip. Next, they drove past the Louvre; Rob couldn't get over how big it was and the length of the queue to get in.

'We'll have to allow for plenty of time if we want to see the Mona Lisa. Look at that queue.'

'I know it looks like a three hour queue but looks can be deceiving mate. I reckon about an hour.'

'Really? We'll see.'

Next they made their way to the far end of the Champs-Elysees and drove along the boulevard until they reached the Arc de Triomphe, which they circuited along with the other hundreds of motor vehicles.

'This is like a dream, Andy. I've travelled extensively for work as you know but no city has impressed me like Paris.'

'This is just the tip of the iceberg. There's plenty more to see.'

'Can hardly wait.'

Andy instructed the taxi driver to take them to their hotel, Le Marais, in the 4th Arrondissement.

They parked outside the hotel admiring the sandstone façade; Andy knew he had picked the right hotel.

They checked in and were shown to their room by a porter who spoke quite good English. Andy asked him for a suggestion for dinner. He recommended Le Bouledoqu just around the corner. They took his recommendation and enjoyed the meal and the ambiance of the quaint Parisian café.

Their days in Paris were filled with visits to the Louvre where they waited in line for just under an hour to gain entry and two hours to view the Mona Lisa. It was decided that the Musee d'Orsay was more enjoyable than the Louvre and the art was magnificent particularly the Monets on show. They now regretted not including Monet's garden at Giverny in their schedule.

They ate in some wonderful restaurants and attended a show at the Moulin Rouge, a very Parisienne experience. They climbed the Eiffel Tower and had a tour through Notre Dame, all in all, a wonderful experience. The next item on their itinerary was the Palace of Versailles.

Versailles

Rob and Andy battled the Paris traffic in the Volkswagen Golf without too much trouble. They both agreed Sydney traffic had nothing on Paris. They picked up the car at ten in the morning hoping they would beat the peak hour but it seemed every hour was peak hour.

Finally they reached the D53, which would take them to Versailles; the trip only took thirty-five minutes allowing for one wrong turn on the outskirts of the city.

The next thirty minutes or so was taken up by searching for a car park, which they finally found about a kilometre from the palace entrance.

The boys were hoping that being September, the crowds would be quite light but unfortunately Asians like to travel to Europe in the autumn.

They got a hint of what was ahead of them by the length of the queue; it stretched out for about five hundred metres; the majority of tourists were Asian.

Finally they bought their tickets and made their way to the entrance.

They decided not to take a guided tour but to use the audio guide through earphones rented from the tourist desk at the entrance to the palace.

It was hard work navigating through the masses; some staterooms were completely blocked by photo-taking visitors.

Once they entered the Hall of Mirrors, any doubts they had about visiting Versailles were dispelled. Rob couldn't get over the opulence. The history relating to the end of World War One and the treaty of Versailles wasn't missed either. It was in this room that the allies ensured it would all happen again twenty years later.

'Andy, I've got to go to the toilet.'

'OK, when we leave the hall, we'll look for one.'

They found a sign leading to the toilets. Rob went in while Andy waited outside. Rob exited the toilets only to be confronted by a huge tour party. He started to panic, as he couldn't see Andy. He turned right when he should have turned left; he was trying to walk quickly but he was going against the throng. As time wore on, his panic levels increased until he began to hyperventilate. A tour guide noticed his condition and offered her assistance. She helped Rob to the office and gave him a glass of water.

'You are obviously lost, sir. Are you here with family or friends?'

'Yes a friend, Andy.'

'OK, I'll put out an announcement on the loud speaker and I'm sure Andy will be here very soon.'

'Thank you.'

Within fifteen minutes Andy arrived at the office. He thanked the guide and took Rob's arm and led him outside into the world-famous gardens. This seemed to settle him and they decided to walk the gardens for a while.

'Andy, I'm getting worried. I would never have panicked eighteen months ago but now my memory is compromised and I've lost all my confidence. I've spent my entire professional career looking for a cure for this bloody disease and now it's come back and bitten me.'

'Mate, you know when we get back home you're undertaking therapy. You're going to beat this bitch, I know it. Just try and relax and stick by me and everything will be all right.'

'I fucking hope so.'

The two travellers found the hire car and set the Satellite Navigation System for Amboise, which was going to be a hundred and sixty mile drive, taking about three hours.

The countryside varied from beautiful to rather boring and they arrived in Amboise at six pm, found their hotel, Le Manoir Les Minimes and checked in. Their expectations for this hotel were well and truly realised.

The following morning they set off to visit their first chateau, Amboise, a fifteenth century chateau with a very colourful history. They could walk to it from their hotel.

In the afternoon the two Francophiles visited Chenonceau and this magnificent chateau nesting in a lake proved to be their favourite.

Two chateaux in a day proved to be their limit so it was decided to visit only two the following day. There were no dramas getting lost or confused; the two partners stuck together the entire day.

They found a lovely little restaurant in Amboise and enjoyed their evening.

The next day took them to Chambord in the morning and Sully-sur-Loire in the afternoon.

Rob was ecstatic; his boyhood dreams had been realised.

Bordeaux

The following morning they travelled to Bordeaux, the famous wine country, which was the part of the trip Andy was looking forward to. Taking a leisurely pace, it took just over six hours to reach the hotel, Les Sources de Caudalie. Although the hotel was only fifteen years old, it used a traditional architectural style and recycled materials. It was conveniently located in the middle of a vineyard.

The next two days were taken up with visiting wineries and their tasting rooms, they tasted and purchased some magnificent wines.

Sarlat was the next port of call, which was only a three-hour drive. Lunch beckoned in the village square.

Sarlat in the Dordogne

They reached their destination right on noon, perfect timing to find "Residence Reygate", a very old villa located within the walls of the medieval town.

They found the old wooden door down a cobbled laneway, which served as the entrance. A key safe with a combination lock had to be opened Andy had the combination which had been emailed by Bernie, the owner, who incidentally lived in Perth Australia.

'This is fantastic, Andy, just look at the stone walls.'

'Sure is, mate, and have a look through the French doors at the outdoor living area. Drinks on the patio at five, I would think.'

'Sounds like a plan to me.'

'OK, let's wander into the village and get ourselves some foie gras on bread and a glass of wine.'

The two travellers enjoyed their lunch, an activity they would repeat often during their stay in this wonderful medieval town.

They could not get over how many ancient castles there were in the region.

Sarlat is located in France's Dordogne department. This region is also known by its ancient name of Perigord. The Perigord is further divided into four distinct regions.

Sarlat is in the Black Perigord (Perigord Noir) where there is an abundance of dense, mainly oak, forests. To the north is the White Perigord (Perigord Blanc), an area riddled with limestone cliffs and caves. Further north again is the Green Perigord (Perigord Vert, filled with rolling farm land and, to the west, is the Purple Perigord (Perigord Pourpre) where there are extensive wine-growing areas.

Their stay finally came to an end after six days; they reluctantly packed the Golf and headed out of Sarlat heading for Nice.

They had chosen Montpellier as their half way stop, a beautiful medieval city that had a reputation for the arts. The Hotel du Parc proved to be as good as the reviews on Trip Advisor had intimated.

After a very French breakfast of pastries, they headed for Nice and a touch of the rich and famous. Arriving at four in the afternoon they found their hotel; Hotel du Petit Palais a small intimate accommodation.

Once checked in, they went for a stroll along the famous esplanade it really was beautiful.

The next two days was spent eating in expensive restaurants and window-shopping, as they couldn't afford what was inside.

They drove the car to the airport and handed it back, next stop Venice.

Venice

The flight from Nice to Venice was only an hour. Once they arrived and picked up their luggage and cleared customs, they walked down to the water's edge and caught a water taxi to their hotel: the Residenza De L'Osmarin. Andy chose it because it was just a five-minute walk to St Mark's Square and ten minutes from the San Zaccaria waterbus stop. It was also a ten-minute stroll to the Rialto Bridge and the markets. When they arrived, they simply alighted from the water taxi and walked into the beautiful reception area.

Their time was spent jostling through the unbelievable throng of tourists to arrive at the Doge's Palace and then wait in a two-hour queue to gain entry.

Coffee in St Mark's square became a daily ritual and using the waterbuses to visit Murano island and a number of other islands was also a regular occurrence.

Finally the day came for their return flight; again they chose to stop over in Dubai to break the trip. By the time they arrived in Sydney they were exhausted. Steve picked them up and drove them to the apartment.

Both Rob and Andy had a further two days of holiday before returning to work; they needed it.

Of Mice and Men

Chapter 12

Rob walked into the lab and greeted his team.

'Hi everybody, I'm back. Have you all been good while I've been away?'

'Of course, with Henry driving us, how could we not be? He's a bigger slave driver than you,' Sophie, the clinical biochemist, joked.

'Well, that's good, I'm pleased to hear it.'

'So, how was the trip?' Henry asked.

'Why don't we wait until lunchtime? I'll give you a complete report. In the meantime I need to meet with Henry and get a briefing.'

The team went back to their workbenches and continued their work Rob and Henry disappeared into Rob's office.

' So how are you feeling, Rob?'

'I'm OK, not fantastic.'

Rob recounted what happened at Versailles.

'You will be pleased to know we have registered even better results with the Alzheimer's mice in the time you were away.'

'In what way?'

' Before you left, the Alzheimer's mice were taking ninety seconds to navigate the maze as opposed to the normal mice taking thirty seconds. With the new treatment given to the affected mice, they have reduced the time down to forty seconds, almost the same time as the normal mice. We believe we can get it down to thirty seconds, completely normal.'

'That's fantastic, mate, so when do you see me beginning the treatment?'

'Very soon, we just need you to complete some tests so we have a measuring tool. We need to be able to monitor your improvement.'

'Of course, so let's do the test.'

'Not so quickly. I've arranged the tests to be conducted in Melbourne for confidentiality purposes. Are you available to fly down this week?' Asked Henry.

'Absolutely.'

Rob flew down on the Thursday; Dr Alan McElroy who knew Rob only by reputation conducted the tests.

The tests were the same as his mother had completed to ascertain her level of the disease.

The retina test was also performed on Rob's eyes. McElroy wanted a belts and braces result.

By the end of the session, Dr McElroy declared that Rob was stage two, heading for stage three.

He knew the results would be positive: he had reconciled himself to the fact.

He flew back to Sydney with some comfort of knowing the new drug had had fantastic results on the mice. He couldn't wait for the treatment to begin; he didn't have to wait long; Henry began his first weekly dosage the following day.

'Rob, I think we should measure your progress on a monthly basis. I'll conduct the retina scan but it's also dependent on you noticing any differences to your memory and other factors such as your confidence levels, etc.'

'That's fine. I'll let you know more regularly than monthly, I can assure you.'

After the first month of treatment, Rob hadn't perceived any noticeable improvement. He knew that the mice also hadn't improved in the first month, so he wasn't too perturbed.

Andy was the biggest problem; everyday at drinks on the balcony, he'd question Rob about the results of the treatment. Finally Rob laid down the law; when there was improvement, Andy would be the first one to know but in the meantime, no questions.

At the end of the second month Rob had noticed an improvement in his memory. At the lab he was remembering forgotten facts. Also, instead of relying on spell checker continually, he was remembering how to spell.

Henry conducted his monthly test and discovered Rob was now at very early stage two Alzheimer's. This was a significant improvement.

'Mate this is a very encouraging result, you should be very pleased.'

'I bloody am! If this keeps continuing I'm home free.'

'Let's just wait until the six months are up but I am very encouraged.'

'How are my little mates going?'

'The mice are still showing signs of improvement, mate. They're on track to being completely normal by the end of the year.'

'Lucky little bastards.'

'Don't worry, Rob, you're on the same track. Maybe not the end of the year but pretty soon after.'

'Well, I'll be able to go home to Andy and give him the good news. He's been on my case for reports and I told him to back off the other day.'

'Why don't you go home early? I'll hold the fort for you.'

'Thanks, mate, but he won't get home from work until six. I might as well stick around here. Thanks again, Henry, for everything.'

'No problem, Rob.'

Life for Rob was pretty normal, as much as his life was ever regarded as normal. He'd catch the ferry across the harbour every weekday and head off to the lab at Woolloomooloo. He'd stop off at The Madagascan Coffee Lounge and get a double shot cappuccino to take away. On the odd occasion, he would buy a Danish pastry.

He was meticulous in his time-keeping, walking into his office at 8.45am every day. His staff could set their watches by him.

It was a Friday when he received a telephone call from his good friend, Stewart Baker Q.C.

'G'day Rob, Stewart here. I've got some good news for you.'

'Hi Stew. What's the news?'

'I've just received a call from the Director of Public Prosecutions. That prick who killed Julian got six years and is banned from driving for life.'

'Good one, he'll have a bit of time on his hands to think about what he did. Stupid bastard. You've made my day, Stewart, thanks for letting me know. I'll announce it at "Happy Hour" tonight.'

Happy Hour began at four thirty every Friday night and apart from having a beer or wine, it also gave Rob the opportunity to make announcements about progress of various projects, staff issues and the like. He called everybody's attention and announced the news about Julian's killer. Instant applause broke out with toasts all around.

When five thirty arrived, Rob bade his farewell to all and made his way home to McMahon's Point.

Andy was already there and beginning to prepare a meal.

'Hi, Andy, how was your day, luv?'

'Yeah, pretty good but bloody busy. How was yours?'

'I had an excellent day. How far are you into cooking dinner?'

'Just peeled a couple of vegies, why?'

'How about I shout you dinner at The Tower?'

'That would be nice but what's the occasion?'

'Pour me a scotch and I'll tell you out on the balcony.'

The two men sat on the outside sofa admiring the magnificent view sipping their drinks. They never tired of this ritual.

Rob recounted the progress he was making with the experimental Alzheimer's cure and the sentence Julian's killer had received.

'Well, that deserves a toast. To you and your speedy recovery and to what's his name, may he rot in jail.'

'Here here.'

Andy and Rob enjoyed their night out with the knowledge Rob was making excellent progress.

Young Doctors in Love

Chapter 13

Steve was enjoying his time at St Vincent's Hospital. It was frantic in the emergency ward particularly in the early hours of the morning when all the drunks poured out of the nightclubs and began fighting or stepping in front of cars. The most common injury Steve treated was stab wounds and concussion. Most of the patients entering the emergency ward were treated and discharged within hours, however the more severe injuries required surgery, and some even resulted in death.

Steve couldn't understand why some of these kids would get drunk and then take vast quantities of illicit drugs like ice. Instead of having a good old time, they would end up in his ward.

One young kid was admitted having been punched in the side of the head by an unknown assailant. He had fallen to the footpath hitting his head on the concrete footpath and was out cold. He never regained consciousness, dying in the ambulance on the way to the emergency ward. He was nineteen, a keen sportsman with an I.Q. of one hundred and forty. He was in his final year of obtaining a law degree. It took just one coward to finish his life and take away his future; Steve was the doctor on duty and was required to pronounce him dead on arrival.

On the same night a more bizarre case came through the E.R. doors. A couple came in together and the man had a blood stained restaurant napkin held against his groin. She had a bandage of sorts wrapped around her head. Steve took them into a treatment room and asked what had happened. Apparently they were celebrating their twelfth month together as a couple and decided they would eat in their favourite restaurant.

She had slipped under the table to deliver his surprise. While she was playing the piccolo she suffered an epileptic fit causing her to clamp down on her boyfriend's penis and wrench it from side to side. In absolute agony and desperate for the torture to stop, he grabbed a fork and stabbed her in the head until she let him go.

They were both treated for their injuries and discharged, however their original plans for the remainder of the evening were curtailed.

In the nine months Steve had been working at St Vincent's, he had established a strong friendship with one of the female doctors, Jackie Hopwood, a tall, very attractive and very capable doctor. They had begun to have coffee together in the canteen and discovered many common areas of interest, including surfing. Jackie grew up in Bondi where her parents owned a very popular restaurant overlooking the ocean. She surfed pretty much every day if the surf was up. At one stage, she contemplated a life as a professional surfer but decided on medicine.

> 'Jackie, would you like to go surfing with me this weekend?'

> 'Sure, where were you thinking?'

> 'Oh just local, Tamarama or Maroubra... maybe Cronulla.'

> 'I think I'd prefer Cronulla for a change. What day?'

> 'Would Sunday suit you? I could pick you up about eight.'

> 'Sounds good, I'm looking forward to it.'

Steve got her address and picked her up in the faithful Kombi, which he called "Nelson".

The surf was really pumping that Sunday and they both enjoyed the session. They ate a late lunch on the esplanade and headed back about five.

The next occasion was far removed from surfing. They attended a concert at the Opera House featuring the Sydney Symphony Orchestra.

Their relationship was growing closer and closer and before long they went on a weekend to Melbourne together to see "War Horse" at the State Theatre in the Arts Centre.

Jackie had a particular interest in the play, as her Great Great Uncle fought and died at a place called Pozieres in Belgium in 1916.

78

Steve enjoyed the show as well; it developed his interest in doing some reading about The Great War.

Coffee and port followed at their hotel, "The Windsor", and then a night of passion followed.

Bondi Attack

Chapter 14

Steve and Jackie's relationship developed into a deep love for each other and although it had proved to be difficult coordinating their shifts, they saw each other twice to three times a week.

Steve had booked a table at their favourite restaurant, "Chiswick", in Paddington for no special reason or that's what he told Jackie. He had purchased a one-carat, brilliant cut diamond ring. The night was to be the night where he would pop the question, as it were.

The two lovers entered the restaurant and were shown to their table.

'I think we should order a bottle of champagne tonight, my love.'

'Really, what's the occasion? Did you get a promotion?'

'No, I just feel like it.'

'If you say so.'

Steve called the waiter over and ordered a bottle of Vintage Veuve Clicquot.

'Well, nothing but the best, hey?'

'You only deserve the best, babe.'

The waiter brought the bottle in a champagne bucket and corked the bottle. He poured Jackie and Steve a glass and left them to it.

'A toast, Jack. To the rest of our lives together.'

'What do you mean?'

Steve pulled the box out of his coat pocket and opened it, showing Jackie the beautiful ring.

'Will you marry me, Jack?'

Jackie was dumbfounded, she hadn't seen it coming.

'I don't know what to say.'

'Say yes.'

'Yes, of course, yes.'

Steve didn't care that they were in a crowded exclusive restaurant; he rose from his chair and kissed her passionately.

The other restaurant patrons gathered what was happening and began to clap. It was a happy occasion for all.

They ate their dinner as if they were both in a dream. They went back to Jackie's apartment in Bondi and opened another bottle of champagne she had been saving in her fridge for a special occasion. You couldn't get more special than this.

The newly engaged couple went to bed and made love for what seemed hours.

Apparently the swells were going to be fantastic the next day so they decided to have a surf at Tamarama before visiting Jackie's parents at the restaurant. Steve intended to ask Peter, Jackie's Dad, for his daughter's hand in marriage. He was a traditionalist.

The surf reports were correct: the waves were rolling in at six feet and barrelling.

The two surfers paddled out together and straddled their surfboards, waiting for the right wave. A set appeared out the back and Steve took the opportunity; he was in the perfect position and rung every ounce out of the wave. He pulled out and began to paddle to catch the next one. When he got out there it was pandemonium, screaming and shouting and surfers banging their hands on the water while others were paddling back to the shore as quickly as they could, hoping for a wave to aid them back.

 He paddled over to a friend and asked him what the fuck was happening.

'Someone has been taken by a shark!'

'Oh no! Who is it? Do you know them, mate?'

'I don't know. I didn't actually see it happen.'

He looked around and couldn't see Jackie.

'She's probably on the beach,' he thought.

Steve paddled over to a bunch of surfers and asked them.

'Did you see it happen?'

'Yeah, she was quite close to me. I thank my lucky stars it wasn't me.

'*She*? It was a girl?'

'Yeah, she's a regular here… bloody hot surfer.'

'Do you know her name?'

'Yeah, Jackie.'

Steve froze. He could do nothing but scream. The few surfers nearby thought it was another shark attack and started paddling frantically to catch a wave, any wave, to get to shore.

The lifesavers were alerted and came out on a jet ski; they hauled Steve aboard and sped him back to the beach. Nobody cared about his surfboard which would be retrieved later. They helped him up to the clubhouse and poured him a whisky to try to settle him down; it didn't. He was inconsolable.

'Mate, is there someone I can call to get you home?'

'I don't know.'

One of Steve's surfing mates offered to drive the Kombi home and contact his brother, Rob.

The trip home was strained; the only words Steve muttered were that he had become engaged the previous night. He also kept muttering it was his fault: he was the one who suggested Tamarama.

Finally they pulled into Steve's car park and his mate, Greg, helped him up and into the apartment. Steve slumped into the couch and began sobbing. Greg used Steve's mobile to call Rob, explaining the situation. Naturally both Rob and Andy were horrified and promised to be there within twenty minutes.

Rob and Andy stayed overnight with Steve and convinced him to stay with them for a while.

The funeral for Jackie was held at St Luke's, Clovelly, only a short distance from Tamarama where she was taken.

All the hospital staff not on duty attended, as did two hundred friends and family.

The eulogy was written and read by her closest and oldest friend Sarah Harris.

A wake was held at her parents' restaurant, "Beyond Bondi". One hundred attended.

Steve did his best to be cordial and accepted people's condolences but it was going to take him a long time before he could get back to a normal life, if ever.

Love Knows No Bounds

Chapter 15

John and Bev attended Jackie's funeral in support of their grieving son. Bev seemed to understand why they were there but became confused at the wake. She thought they were there to party, drink lots of wine and gorge on the delicious food. John had to keep a close eye on her but at one stage had to go to the men's room. When he returned, Bev was drinking white wine from the bottle. He quickly asked if he could share it with her and discreetly hid it away.

Life was progressively getting more difficult for John; Bev had progressed to stage five and, as he expected, became easily confused about pretty well everything from dressing appropriately to knowing what day it was. He now had to dress her each day and prepare all the meals. Bev loved her wine. John had to limit her or she would become blind drunk and end up on the floor doing herself an injury. She still loved visits from her sons and had no difficulty recognising them, although she always seemed to have trouble determining who Andy was and how he fitted in, despite having known him for several years.

John decided that it would be beneficial if they took a trip to Melbourne as it would give Bev the opportunity of catching up with some old friends and visit places they used to frequent when they lived there. He was quite prepared to accept the fact that she may well not remember anyone, including her two sisters, despite the fact she spoke to them regularly on the telephone.

He asked Rob and Steve what they thought of the idea when they visited their parents at their apartment.

'I'm thinking of driving your mother to Melbourne and try stimulating her memory by catching up with Auntie Alice and Auntie Barbara along with a few old friends. What do you think Steve?'

'Dad, nothing will stimulate Mum's memory. Unless we can discover a cure, there's no going back.'

'Even so, mate, I think it would do her the world of good. You, too, for that matter,' Steve said enthusiastically.

'What route are you thinking of taking Dad?'

'I've printed it out today, I'll get it.'

John showed the boys the suggested itinerary provided by the travel site.

Day 1: Sydney to Jervis Bay (196km, 3 hours 5 minutes)

Start your coastal village experience straight away and take the Grand Pacific scenic and Sea Cliff Bridge to the bustling coastal city of Wollongong Continue on to beautiful Kiama where the famous blowhole awaits. Follow the coastline through lush rolling hills to Gerringong and Gerroa, perched on the cliffs above the ocean, overlooking Seven Mile Beach. From here, follow the Grand Pacific Drive alongside the Shoalhaven River. Take in the shops and cafes at Berry before taking the turnoff to Jervis Bay in time for a late afternoon swim or surf.

Day 2: Jervis Bay to Narooma
(186km, 2 hours 40 minutes)

Jervis Bay is well known for its resident dolphin population, which can be seen on a dolphin and whale cruise with Dolphin Watch Cruises. The local beaches along the bay are famous for their white sand and turquoise waters – Hyam's Beach is reputed to have the whitest sand in the world. Travel south stopping for lunch at Bateman's Bay where you can enjoy take-away fish and chip, sitting on the dock of the bay. Take time to discover the Batemans

Marine Park where the recreational fishing is superb and on to the coastal village of Narooma and gateway to the National Park's Montague Island.

Day 3: Narooma to Mallacoota
(213km, 3 hours 25 minutes)

Visit the well-preserved villages of Central Tilba and Tilba Tilba where you can shop for high quality local arts and crafts, food and wine. Continue to Bermagui and travel along the beach road to Mimosa Rocks National Park for a picnic lunch and swim in the lagoons or continue on to surf Tathra Beach. Stop off in Pambula for fresh oysters. Continue on across the border into Victoria, to Gypsy Point and Mallacoota Hire a boat at Mallacoota and tie up at one of the barbeque jetties in the magnificent Croajingolong National Park.

Day 4: Mallacoota to Metung
(219km, 2 hours 55 minutes)

Feed the sea eagles on a morning boat trip from Gipsy Point Travel south to Cape Conran Coastal Park for a picnic lunch. Continue towards Lakes Entrance, both a picturesque holiday town and fishing fleet port. Arrive at the stylish Metung in time for a late afternoon sail or motor yacht cruise around Australia's largest inland waterway. Enjoy dinner at one of the town's fine restaurants.

Day 5: Meting to Wilsons Promontory
(277km, 4 hours)

Have breakfast early and call in at Yarram for lunch on the way to _Wilsons Promontory_ National Park located at the Australian mainland's southernmost point and famous for its flora and fauna, wild ocean beaches and mountain views. Set up camp or book into *accommodation at Tidal River or nearby Yanakie, Walkerville South or Forster Choose from the many walks, including the trail to Squeaky Beach with its pure white quartz sand or the walk up Mt Oberon for a great panoramic view. As you move around the park look out for kangaroos, birds, echidnas, wombats and other wildlife.*

Day 6: Wilsons Promontory to Phillip Island (137km, 2 hours 35 minutes)

Stop for coffee at quirky Fish Creek, a tiny township alive with arts, crafts, books and cafes or shop at one of the great restaurants in Inverloch for lunch. Cross the bridge onto Phillip Island, a popular family holiday destination. Experience Churchill Island, a working heritage farm, during the warmer months, see one of Australia's largest fur seal colonies up close and personal with Wildlife Coast Cruise and don't miss the daily dusk parade of little penguins as they parade up the beach.

Day 7: Phillip Island to Mornington Peninsula (111km, 2 hours)

View Australia's favourite furry friends at the Koala Conservation Centre on specially raised boardwalks, before making your way back across the bridge to San Remo and onto the highway toward Mornington Peninsular While on the peninsula, go for stimulating walks, dine in excellent restaurants and taste the regional wines on offer at over 50 cellar doors.

Day 8: Mornington Peninsula to Melbourne (69km, 1 hour 5 minutes)

Visit Moonlight Sanctuary at Pearcedale where you can get up close to Australia's unique wildlife and check out some of the peninsula's championship golf courses. The end of this journey takes you into Melbourne, Australia's second largest city, famous

*for events, sport, cafe culture, art and an amazing array of cuisine
to please any palate.*

'Of course we won't be doing all the things they suggest but a leisurely drive along the coast would be far better for Mum rather than screaming down the Hume Highway in twelve hours.'

'Yeah I think it would be a good break for both of you. Have you told Mum yet?' Rob asked.

'No, I don't think I will until we begin our trip. It would only confuse her.'

'I think you're right, Dad.' Steve agreed.

The day arrived to begin the journey; John packed their suitcases and loaded them into the Audi Q5.

He made sure there were plenty of lollies as Bev loved eating them in the car. He also ensured the iPod dock was working, as music was also an essential part of any road journey.

'Bev, darling, we're going for a drive. Are you ready?'

'Yes, darling, where are we going?'

'Oh, I thought we might drive to Melbourne for a change.'

'Don't be silly, John, where are we really going?'

'It's a surprise, my love.'

'Good! I like surprises.'

'Well come on, let's go.'

John was surprised that his wife didn't question why he was packing their suitcases and taking them down to the car. 'Just another part of dementia', he thought.

Once they got through the Sydney traffic, they headed down to Jervis Bay, driving along the Grand Pacific Highway. They passed beautiful beaches where the sand was white and the ocean was indigo blue. John thought Bev might like to stop and see the Blowhole at Kiama, south of Wollongong.

They walked down to the spot where they could get the best view.

'Well, where is it John?'

'It will blow any minute, hon, just wait.'

'It's not happening. Let's go.'

Then, an almighty roar sounded and water spurted up as high as a two storey building. After the initial shock, Bev couldn't stop laughing. She loved it.

They reached their destination, Jervis Bay, about four in the afternoon and checked into "Jervis Bay Haven" a self-contained cottage with magnificent views across the water. John had decided that they would stay in self-contained accommodation throughout the trip so Bev didn't have to cope with other residents at breakfast etc.

Bev tended to go to bed early, about 7.30pm, leaving John to either watch television or read. Just before setting out on the trip he watched a program called "Terry Pratchett, Living with Alzheimer's" The program really moved him, as did Terry. In 2007 Pratchett had been diagnosed with early onset Alzheimer's. He was a very successful author, so successful in fact that he was the second biggest selling author in the U.K. after J.K. Rowling.

John decided to purchase a couple of Pratchett's books to take away with him on the trip; he thought it might give him a better insight into how someone like Pratchett coped with this horrible affliction. The books he chose were *Raising Steam* and *Snuff* from the Disc World Series.

It gave John great hope that Terry Pratchett was still writing books albeit with dictation software rather than a keyboard, which he could no longer operate.'If Pratchett can do it why not Bev?' he thought.

He began to believe that Bev with her innate intelligence could begin to keep a diary, which may one day become a book about her experiences with Alzheimer's.

89

He acknowledged to himself that this was a very optimistic view but nevertheless where there's hope…

The following morning they left for Narooma, a few hours down the coast road; as they were travelling they noticed several motor vehicles on the side of the road with people looking out to sea, some with binoculars. John also pulled over to investigate.

A pod of humpback whales was migrating south; they were quite close to the shore and easily visible to the whale watchers. The beautiful creatures fascinated Bev. Some years ago, John and Bev had a holiday on Fraser Island and had gone out on one of the many whale-watching boats.

The two travellers watched as whales passed; they stood there on the bluff for a good half an hour.

Bev could not stop talking about the experience until they reached their destination. John was delighted that she had experienced something that brought back memories of her visit to Fraser Island.

They checked into their beach side cottage and decided to have fish and chips sitting on the pier. John and Bev relished the scenery and the magnificent fish and chips; they returned to the cottage and drank a glass of wine on the veranda watching the sunset.

John was amazed and at the same time confused; Bev could remember a holiday twenty years ago yet forget what she did last week or yesterday for that matter.

Apparently that was the nature of the beast; most people with dementia remember the distant past more clearly than recent events. This is because memories tend to decline in reverse order to when they were experienced. People will often have difficulty remembering what happened a few minutes or hours ago, but can recall, in detail, life when they were much younger. However, as the condition progresses, even these long-term memories will eventually decline.

They retired to bed about nine pm; one interesting side benefit John found was that Bev's sex drive had increased dramatically. In her mind, 'bed' meant sex. This was markedly different from their sex life prior to Alzheimer's, where 'bed' meant sleep, except for the odd occasion.

The next step in their coastal odyssey was Lakes Entrance, a picturesque coastal town over the border in Victoria. They enjoyed lunch there then motored on to Metung where they would be spending the night in yet another delightful cottage overlooking the largest inland waterway in Australia.

John was enjoying *Raising Steam* which was not the sort of book he would normally read. He read Tolkien's *Lord of the Rings* when he was at university but tended to read non-fiction throughout his adult life. Nevertheless, the way Pratchett wrote made the story exciting and he had no trouble in reading it. John certainly built a great respect for Terry Pratchett and it gave him hope for his wife.

Over the next few days they travelled through Wilson's Promontory and on to Philip Island where Bev was delighted to see the Fairy Penguins.

Their last night on the road was spent in a beautiful apartment called 'Aquabelle' overlooking the sea.

The next day they drove into Melbourne where they would be staying with Bev's sister, Barbara, in the leafy suburb of Kew.

John drove the Audi into the driveway and beeped the horn to signal their arrival, whereupon Barbara and her husband, Alan, came out to greet them. There were hugs and kisses all around and although Bev seemed to recognise her sister, John had his doubts.

They all moved inside and Barbara made tea and brought out the scones she had baked that morning.

'Well, Bev, you look wonderful. How are you feeling, darling?'

'I feel fine although I've got Alzheimer's. Did you know that?'

'Yes, darling, I knew that.'

'I remember you, though, you're Alice aren't you?'

'I'm Barbara, sweetheart. Alice is your younger sister.'

'Oh, fuck it.'

'Don't be upset. You knew I was your sister. You just got the names mixed up.'

91

'I suppose so. I know I'm getting worse, that's the hard thing.'

'Well, hon, at least you have John to support you.'

'I suppose so, although he doesn't do much.'

'I think you'll find he does a lot.'

'Yes, he's quite wonderful. So where is Alice?'

'She'll be here shortly. She's coming with her daughter, Sophie. You haven't seen her for a long time.'

'I haven't seen anybody for a long time.'

Bev and her sister started talking about their childhood and the wonderful holidays the family spent at Phillip Island. The family had owned a beach house on the bay side of the island. The girls were all very competent horsewomen and took every opportunity to ride across the island and the pristine white beaches on their horses.

Bev remembered these times and could laugh about what she and her sisters got up to when they were on holidays at the island.

Barbara was bemused by Bev's long-term memory of her childhood yet she couldn't remember the most simple of things, things like where she lived and what her career had been.

Alice and Sophie arrived and made a fuss over Bev, complimenting her on her outfit and how young she looked. Bev was enjoying all the attention and responded very favourably. When things settled down they all sat around the large timber table in the beautiful country kitchen. Barbara made a pot of tea and everything seemed to be going well until Bev made a comment to Sophie.

'Well, dear you're a lucky girl. Hired help don't normally get to have tea with their employers.'

'Auntie Bev, I'm not hired help. I'm your niece.'

'Excuse me, I don't have a niece.'

'You have four nieces, darling,' Barbara responded.

'Rubbish, absolute rubbish! I'd remember if I had a fucking niece or not.'

'OK, let's just drop it for now,' an embarrassed Alice responded.

The two sisters and Sophie tried to keep the conversation going but it was futile. Barb suggested Bev take a 'nanna nap' before dinner, so she did.

John walked into the kitchen just as Bev was being led to the guest bedroom. Barbara briefed him on what had happened and he just shook his head and muttered 'Yeah, what can you do? Poor thing.'

David, Barbara's husband, had planned a family dinner that night and their three daughters were coming over with their respective partners and children. She hoped it would be a happy occasion with no drama. Everybody was fully aware of Bev's condition so they knew they could expect unusual behaviour.

The dinner was a great success. Bev seemed to enjoy herself and John monitored her wine intake. John had developed a cunning plan to minimise any problems with Bev's drinking. He half filled a white wine bottle with water, and as she didn't notice, the alcohol intake was dramatically limited. Bev also enjoyed a Scotch; John did the same with the whisky. She had water with drink so the actual amount of Scotch was minimal. In this way John could feel comfortable with the amount she consumed.

The next big task was to meet up with three of Bev's oldest friends at a restaurant in South Yarra, a trendy inner city location.

John and Bev arrived first; this, John thought, would be the best way for Bev to settle in, ready to greet her friends rather than arriving last and being overwhelmed.

The waiter showed them their table and asked if they would like a drink while they waited for the rest of the party to arrive. John had phoned the restaurant and asked for his special wine to be available; he had explained Bev's Alzheimer's.

John ordered a red wine and Bev a white. All was going to plan so far.

He had organised the three friends to arrive at five minute intervals so Bev could take it all in. First to enter the restaurant was Mary

Gilford who had worked with Bev in the law practice for over ten years.

'Bev, hello darling, you look absolutely amazing.'

'Hello.'

'It must be three years since we saw each other. Where was it? I know, it was at the opening of French Impressionists exhibition at the National Gallery.'

'Was it? I wouldn't really know, you see I've got Alzheimer's. Did you know that?'

'John did tell me, sweetheart, but you would hardly know.'

'Really, well that's good,' Bev said with a sarcastic tone.

The other two friends, Rachel, an old university friend and Emma, a horse-riding friend, arrived at their allocated times. The reaction from Bev was quite different from when Mary had arrived. She was friendly and seemed to recognise them both.

John had seen this before. Bev could be aloof with one, and charming in her own way to another.

In general, John concluded that it had all been worthwhile and it did exercise Bev' memory which was the purpose of the exercise.

The Melbourne trip had been a great success overall, including the drive along the coastal road, however it was time to return to Sydney. This time they took the Hume Highway and had just one overnight stop at Albury.

They arrived back in Sydney in the late afternoon and had a take-away Chinese meal then went to bed. Bev was too tired to have sex, much to John's relief.

The usual regime began next morning; John would rise first and make Bev a coffee. He would then prepare breakfast, usually a bowl of fruit and yogurt followed by toast and tea.

John would then shower her while she sat in a plastic chair, as her balance wasn't particularly good. He dried her and dressed her in a tracksuit. He also dressed in his tracksuit and they would walk for about forty minutes up hill and down dale. The doctor had advised him that regular exercise was very good for her condition.

On returning to the apartment, the devoted husband had to shower her again. Bev refused to go for a walk without first showering and when she returned, she was 'all hot and sweaty', or so she said.

By the time the morning regime was complete, it was ten thirty, time for an outing.

John would drive to Chatswood and the two of them would walk around the mall or go to Bunnings Hardware or just drive up to Manly. Bev didn't care, as long as she was out of the apartment.

After lunch, which quite often consisted of MacDonald's, not so much for the quality of the food but so Bev could watch the young children in the play area, Bev would have her afternoon sleep.

The remainder of the afternoon was spent watching soapies on television. John took this time to read in his study or pay bills etc.

Not a very exciting life.

Trials and Tribulations
Chapter 16

Rob had entered his fourth month of the trial and was seeing significant benefits. The procedure was that Henry was the only person who had access to the drugs; he did not want Rob to have the temptation of increasing the dose in the hope that he would be cured sooner.

Each Monday at 10 AM Henry would enter Rob's office and suggest they have a coffee down the road. In actual fact they would go to Henry's car where Rob would receive an injection of what they both called the "Alzheimer's bomb."

The Monday following the bomb they would review Rob's progress by some simple mathematical tests and the retina test. On each of these occasions Henry was amazed at the progress being made. He now felt confident that Rob would be completely cured by the end of the six-month trial.

They would then need to get the team working on commercialising the drug so that others could be cured. Henry nor Rob were sure if someone with progressed Alzheimer's would benefit from the treatment but Rob was keen to begin a trial with his mother. Henry was in agreement.

'Henry, apart from curing Alzheimer's, do you know the other implications?'

'What implications, mate?'

'The implication of the company making hundreds of million dollars.'

'Well, yeah, sure I had thought of that. I try not to think about it but our success bonus would be well over a million dollars each. In fact the team will all take home a significant bonus.

Anyway, as you said we shouldn't think about the money. It's your health we need to concentrate on.'

'When do you think I should speak to my Dad about Mum starting a program?'

'Let's wait another month. It will be five months then and I think if all goes to plan we should be very confident of success.'

'OK.'

The next month came and the usual procedures were followed and the usual tests were completed.

'Well, mate, I'll put my neck out and say you're fucking cured.'

Rob grabbed Henry and gave him the biggest hug and kissed him on the cheek.

'You beauty! Now I can be confident I have a fucking future with my work, with Andy, with my family. I can't believe it. This is better than winning the lottery. The only down side is, I can't tell anybody, well… apart from Andy. Oh well, doesn't matter.'

When things settled down, Rob went back to his office and rang Andy, the only person he could tell.

'Mate, put some champagne on ice when you get home.'

'Why? Did you get a rise or something?'

'I'll reveal all when I get home.'

'Sounds promising, OK.'

Now the two men could get on with their lives without the fear of Alzheimer's hanging over their heads.

Rob arrived home to the apartment at 6.30pm as usual; Andy had the Moet in an ice bucket on the balcony waiting for the good news.

'Well, come on Rob, what's the news that deserves Moet?'

'I am completely cured.'

'Far out! That's fantastic man! Whoa, I can't believe it.'

'Even though there's another month in the trial, Henry signed me off as being cured.'

'I think I'm going to cry, mate. I thought the remainder of our lives would be me visiting you in a nursing home. Now we can do all the things we planned.'

'I'm going to put my hand up for what we should do now.'

'What? Anything! I'm with you, bud.'

'Let's go back to Europe next holidays.'

'Yeah, great idea. When are you due for your next lot?'

'I've still got four weeks up my sleeve. Why don't we say June?'

'That's only three months away but hey, why not? Let's do it.'

Rob and Andy finished the champagne and sat down to a dinner of ravioli and a fine bottle of red. They didn't stop talking about their European trip.

Alone

Chapter 17

Steve was having real trouble coping without Jackie. He had lived and breathed for her, they had talked about starting their own medical centre. They also talked about starting a family: it was going to be wonderful. Now all he had in his life was loneliness, a complete void.

It wasn't too bad when he was at work. The emergency centre didn't give you time to think about yourself. You treated one stabbing case and another was wheeled in straight away.

It was when he went home to his empty apartment that it really hit him. Photos of Jackie were everywhere and her clothes were still hanging up in his wardrobe. Even though Jackie had her own place, she tended to stay at Steve's on her days off, which accounted for her clothes taking more space than his own.

He would pour himself a scotch and sit out on the balcony and contemplate committing suicide. He knew he would never go through with it but nevertheless his depression was severe. Finally he decided to visit a doctor, someone he didn't know and get prescribed an anti- depressant. This seemed to help eliminate his death wish but there was still the chronic loneliness.

He was talking to a friend at the hospital about his situation and she recommended meditation. She explained that when she lost her mother and father in a car crash she began to meditate to try and cope with the tragedy. Her name was Kate Wilson and she was a radiologist. Kate suggested that Steve accompany her to her meditation classes, which he agreed to do. At first it all seemed a bit Maharishi-Yogi-Beatles to him but as he learnt the method, an inner calm did come over him when he entered a deep meditation. He liked the place it took him to and he continued attending the classes with Kate for the remainder of the year. When the class broke up for

Christmas he was quite devastated so Kate suggested they continue together at his apartment until classes resumed in February.

Kate and Steve started to create a strong bond with meditation as the glue. After the session they would go out to dinner and talk and talk and talk. Conversation was not a problem between these two friends. The relationship transformed from friendship to love over the following twelve months. Jackie had been gone two years and Steve felt he was ready for another relationship. Kate had always been ready as she had always liked Steve.

Steve was opening his mail expecting more bills when an envelope from the John Hopkins Hospital grabbed his attention. In essence he had been invited to work at the hospital in San Francisco for a twelve-month period. Doctors who were regarded as outstanding were invited each year from around the world. This was an opportunity Steve could not refuse. It would really enhance his career but how to tell Kate? He decided he would take her out to their favourite restaurant and tell her there. She wouldn't yell at him in a crowded restaurant, he figured.

'I love coming here, Steve. Is there any special reason why you chose Rock Pool?'

Kate was hoping a small box would be taken out of his pocket.

'Well, darling, I do have something to tell you.'

'Do you, well what is it then?'

'I have received an invitation to take up a position at John Hopkins Hospital in Maryland, USA.'

'What, for how long?'

'Twelve months.'

'I see and what do you expect me to do for a year?'

'Kate, it's not a life sentence.'

'Maybe not for you, swanning around America and having a good old time while I'm expected to wait dutifully for my boyfriend to return.'

'No, you're not.'

'What do you mean?'

'I want you to marry me and we'll go together.'

'You're kidding.'

'No I'm not, my love. Will you marry me?'

'Yes! My God, of course I'll marry you.'

Kate jumped up and went around to Steve's side of the table, thrust her arms around him and kissed him passionately.
This all seemed a little like déjà vu to Steve.

'So, when do we leave?'

'Next January.'

'My God, it's September now. We can't possibly organise a wedding and sub-lease our apartments in that time.'

'Yes we can. It doesn't have to be a Royal wedding, just something small and simple.'

'OK, but we better get started.'

'Oh I nearly forgot.'

Steve reached into his pocket and pulled out a small box. He opened it, displaying a beautiful classic diamond ring. He removed it from its box and slipped it on Kate's left ring finger.

'It's beautiful, Steve, I love it.'

'Right then. It's official: we're engaged.'

The restaurant patrons began to clap but the young couple had taken no notice whether anybody in the restaurant was aware of the proposal taking place. They now acknowledged the applause and Kate held her hand up with the newly acquired engagement ring for all to see.

Steve had suffered deep trauma and a depression he thought would never end after Jackie's death. Now he was in an entirely different space. He believed he had a future and it included Kate.

Hope Eternal

Chapter 18

Rob had regained his confidence; from the time he was diagnosed he had asked Henry to make the monthly presentation to the board on the progress the team was making with AL252, the code name of the Alzheimer's cure. He now made the presentation with the support of other team members including Henry.

He found his sense of humour again and really began to enjoy life. His work rate had also increased and he was getting great results. All in all he was back to being Rob.

He had retained his memory of what life was like suffering from the dreaded "Big A" and it gave him a stronger empathy for people suffering the affliction, including his mother.

He asked Henry to join him at the "Arabic" coffee lounge where they frequented when keen to get out of the lab.

'Mate, I have something I wish to discuss with you.'

'Yes, mate, what's on your mind?'

'Remember I told you about my mother and asked you about the treatment?

Well, I've been thinking that AL252 may be of some benefit to her. I know she is far more advanced than I was but even if she experiences some improvement, it would be worth it.'

'Well, mate, as you say, she is quite advanced. What stage is she at now?'

'Stage five.'

'As you know, Rob, there aren't any guarantees. This may or may not work on her but then again, she can't get any worse.

I'm willing to start her on a course over the next three months and then we will need to assess her progress.'

'Fantastic, Henry, I really do appreciate your support. I need to discuss this with my Dad first but I'm sure he will be in agreement.'

'OK, mate, let me know when you want me to start the program.'

Rob rang his Father and suggested he come around for a chat. John was curious as to why, but naturally agreed.

Rob brought a bottle of fine red and he and his father settled into the leather wingbacks in John's study. John had never counted the books housed in this beautiful intimate room but he estimated there would be over two thousand. Bev was already in bed despite the time being seven in the evening.

'Dad, I've got something to tell you. Please don't interrupt me, I'll answer all your questions when I'm done.'

'OK what is it?'

Rob explained that he had been diagnosed with Familial Alzheimer's disease twelve months ago. He went on to describe events such as the visit to Versailles and how it had affected his research.

'Holy shit, how do you cope? I know what it has been like with your mother.'

'Dad, you promised to listen without interruption.'

'OK, but fucking hell, son.'

'I, along with Henry and a small team, have been working on finding a cure for Alzheimer's. We believe we have found it.

We have been able to tailor treatments which will target the toxic plaques that clump together in the brain and cause confusion and memory loss. We have achieved this by working out how an enzyme triggers the destruction of neurons in the brain. We have obtained extraordinary knowledge about how the enzyme gamma secretase can be modulated. This knowledge has proved to be invaluable for developing even better targeted drugs to fight the disease.'

'That all sounds fantastic Rob but are you really sure it will work?'

'Well it worked on the laboratory mice and it worked on me.'

'You mean it's been approved by the Therapeutic Goods Administration?'

'Not exactly, Dad.'

'What do you mean, Rob. Did you experiment on yourself?'

'With the help of Henry; we had seen how the Alzheimer's-induced mice reacted for about twelve months so consequently we were confident it would work with humans i.e. me. Dad, I knew I only had a few years left before I ended up in a nursing home. I felt it was worth the risk. If I hadn't taken the risk, I wouldn't be having an intelligent conversation with you now.'

'I suppose I would have done the same thing, despite my drug company background. The most important thing, Rob, is you are cured.'

'I would like to put Mum on the same program with your approval of course.'

'Do you really think it would make any difference, Rob? Your mother has recently been diagnosed as stage six and you know what that means.'

'Well, it couldn't hurt and if it improves her condition, you and she will enjoy a better life. Mate, wouldn't you like her to be staying up with you until ten rather than going off to bed at seven?'

'Of course I would and I wish I could have a reasonable conversation with her. I miss going out to a restaurant or the theatre with her.' Tears were welling up and he looked away from his son.

'So then let's do it, let's get started.'

'When?'

'Tomorrow is as good a time to start as any.'

'Why not?'

Rob sat with his father and finished the bottle of Shiraz, reminiscing about the good times and discussing the possibilities of the future.

At eleven Rob left, excited about the prospect of curing Bev or at least improving her condition.

He met with Henry the next morning and Rob briefed him on the meeting the previous evening.

'You don't have to come with me; I'm more than capable of administering a needle.'

'No, Rob, I think it's important that we both be there. Remember, what we're doing is as illegal as was your program. We started this thing together and we'll finish it together.'

'Thanks, mate, you really are a true friend.'

The two research scientists arranged with John to be at the apartment at six in the evening. Bev was looking at them with bewilderment; she sort of recognised Rob but who was this other person?

'Right, Mum, I'm going to give you a little injection.'

'I hate injections, piss off!'

'Mum, it's for your own good. You don't want to get a nasty flu and be sick in bed for weeks, do you?'

'John, tell them to go away.'

'Bev, darling, it's for the best. It won't take long.'

'Oh, alright, get on with it.'

Rob injected his mother with AL252 in the upper left arm.

'Shit, that hurt. You said it wouldn't hurt, you bastard.'

John shook his head, Bev hardly swore before Alzheimer's; now she was up there with the best of them.

Rob and Henry explained to John that they would need to return each week and administer the drug. If Bev were going to improve, it

105

would show up after about three months. John bade the two friends farewell and returned only to find Bev drinking red wine from a bottle in the kitchen.

'God, I hope this works,' he thought.

Not Born in the USA

Chapter 19

Steve was beginning to wind down in preparation for his wedding and subsequent move to America. Most of the wedding planning was Kate's responsibility as was preparing for the trip. Steve's tasks were selling his surfboard and arranging for the Kombi to be held in storage. To be fair he also had to arrange his best man, which would be Rob.

Finally the day arrived and, as in most weddings, it was bedlam before the vows were taken. Kate's first task was to get her hair done, along with the bridesmaid, Emma. It was not going to plan. The hairdresser could not get Jackie's hair to behave the way she had hoped. Eventually it all worked out and she looked beautiful with magnificent hair and makeup complimented by a t-shirt and jeans.

Steve and Rob had a much easier time of it; they had breakfast at Neutral Bay: bacon and eggs and double shot cappuccinos then went back to Steve's apartment to get dressed.

'Now, Rob, don't forget the ring. I have noticed you have been a little forgetful lately.'

'Yeah, ain't that the truth, mate? Steve, I think it's time I told you about what's been going on in my life over the last year or so.'

Rob told his brother about contacting Alzheimer's and the illegal cure he had administered. Steve was shocked but also relieved his brother had won through.

'I'm gobsmacked, mate. I had no idea, apart from the obvious memory lapses. I just put that down to the stress at the lab.'

'I've started Mum on the same program, we're hoping she will show some signs of improvement.'

'Mum! Surely she's too far progressed.'

'We don't know but it's got to be worth a try.'

'Who's we?'

'Henry, my 2IC, at the Lab.'

'So he's in on it?'

'Without him I wouldn't be cured.'

'What about Dad?'

'Of course he is. We wouldn't begin the program without his approval.'

'Of course, mate, sorry.'

'Well now that you know, let's forget it as they say and get you hitched.'

Rob and Steve caught a taxi to the little church at Neutral Bay where about thirty people were waiting.

'This is your last chance to pull out, mate. After this, your life is no longer your own.'

'That's OK with me. I couldn't be happier marrying Kate. After Jackie died I really didn't think there could be anyone to replace her; that is until I met Kate.'

The two brothers acknowledged the group of friends and their parents as well as Kate's as they walked down the aisle to wait for his bride.

The music began: "Reign of Love" by Coldplay, not the traditional "Here Comes the Bride". Kate began the slow walk down the aisle on the arm of her very proud father, Sam.

She looked beautiful in a slim-fitting white wedding dress and sheer veil.

The minister began the service, which ended with a prolonged kiss.

They walked down the aisle arm in arm, accepting their friends' and family's best wishes.

The reception was held in a small restaurant at Balmoral Beach overlooking the harbour.

There was plenty of wine, excellent food and the bare minimum of speeches. There were no telegrams or emails.

After a weekend away at Nelson Bay, they were back home preparing to leave for America the following week. A long honeymoon would have to wait.

Rob and Andy drove them to the airport and bade them farewell. Neither Steve nor Kate was looking forward to the sixteen-hour flight in economy class. Steve arranged a bottle of strong sleeping pills to try and ease the burden.

Once they had eaten their delicious economy class meal, they popped their pill; the next thing they knew, breakfast was being served. The pill had done its job.

They flew directly into San Francisco International airport by-passing the mayhem of LAX. Their plan was to spend a week in San Francisco, a city on both their bucket lists. It was highly unlikely they could get there once they were living in Maryland.

They caught a cab to the hotel, The Mark Twain, a four star hotel and more than adequate for their needs.

Steve had a free week before he was due to start at the hospital, so Kate and he used that time very effectively. The first thing on their list was a tour of Alcatraz, which they enjoyed despite the morose nature of the island. The two cells, which grabbed their imaginations, were that of Al Capone and the "Birdman".

The next day was a tour to see the giant redwood trees; they crossed the Golden Gate and proceeded to the national park. Kate couldn't believe the size of the trees, whereas Steve was more impressed with the lunch on the way back at Sausalito, a beautiful fishing village on the bay.

The rest of their free time was spent eating seafood chowder at Fisherman's Wharf and catching the cable car. They also snuck in some shopping for warm winter clothes as it gets very cold in Baltimore.

On the following Monday, the two newly-weds flew out to Baltimore, about a three-hour flight. Steve was due to start his tenure at the hospital on the Wednesday. Kate did not have a job arranged and without the correct visa, couldn't work in the United States.

It didn't seem quite fair that illegal immigrants were coming across the border in droves and securing work, yet she was prohibited from working.

She decided she would take on some postgraduate study online and she enrolled with Sydney University to undertake a Masters of Medical Radiology.

Steve arrived at the John Hopkins nice and early, as he had no idea where the administration wing was located. Having asked a doctor for directions, he arrived in the building at 8.45am, fifteen minutes early.

On the stroke of nine, a very distinguished man entered the auditorium where the young doctors had been seated, twenty in all.

'Good morning, ladies and gentlemen, my name is Dr Charles Manning. I am the head of medicine at this very illustrious hospital. I am sure you have all done your research on the history of the establishment but I don't care: I'm going to tell you anyway.'

The doctors gave a polite chuckle.

'The University was founded on January 22, 1876, and named for its benefactor, the philanthropist, John Hopkins. Daniel Gilman was inaugurated as the first president on February 22, 1876.

This institution pioneered the concept of the modern research university in the United States and we have been ranked among the world's top such universities throughout our history. The National Science Foundation (NSF) has ranked John Hopkins number one among U.S. academic institutions in total science, medical and engineering research and development for thirty-one consecutive years

110

As of 2011, thirty-seven Nobel Prize winners have been affiliated with John Hopkins over the course of 120 years. The university's research has been ranked as the third most cited of any institution globally, earning it a far-reaching reputation as one of the most prestigious universities in the world.

We now maintain campuses in Maryland and Washington, D.C. along with international centres in Italy, Malaysia, China and Singapore. The university is organized into two undergraduate divisions and five graduate divisions on two main campuses — the Homewood campus and the Medical Institutions campus — both located in Baltimore. As you all well know, the university also consists of various other schools.

The portrait of our founder is on the wall above my head, a fine figure of a man.

On his death in 1873, John Hopkins, a Quaker and childless bachelor, bequeathed seven million dollars ($1.6 billion in 2014 dollars) to fund a hospital and university in Baltimore, Maryland. At that time this fortune, generated primarily from the Baltimore and Ohio Railroad was the largest philanthropic gift in the history of the United States.

So, you young doctors will have the best learning, the best facilities and the best opportunity to advance your careers.

I believe we have representatives from Australia, China, Singapore, Italy and Great Britain. Make the most of the next twelve months and your careers will flourish.

You would have noticed the schedules placed on your seats. Go to your assigned departments and begin to learn. Good morning, ladies and gentlemen.'

Steve, along with his fellow scholarship winners, was excited by the opportunities but also under no delusion that the next twelve months were going to be hard work.

Kate was also under no delusions the next twelve months were going to be tough but a Masters at the end of it would make it all worthwhile.

Steve had been assigned to the head of neurology, Dr Adam Russell, one of the most respected brain surgeons in the country. Initially Steve would observe an operation but eventually Dr Russell invited him to be part of the team. This gave Steve an incredible opportunity to hone his surgical skills under the eye of a master albeit in a very limited way. Dr Russell had completed thirteen years of post-secondary education. Steve would need to study for a further five years' residency if he wished to become a brain surgeon.

Kate was enjoying studying for her Masters; her professor at Sydney University, Dr Adam Wilcox, had taken a real interest in his student residing in Baltimore. He had arranged with John Hopkins Medical School to permit her to complete her prac. work using the school's radiology equipment.

Both Kate and Steve looked forward to their weekends after such intensive working weeks.

Baltimore was renowned for its urban redevelopment, including its historical harbour precinct.

They both picked the Walters Art Museum as their first port of call.

"The Walters Art Museum in Baltimore, Maryland is internationally renowned for its collection of art. The collection presents an overview of world art from pre-dynastic Egypt to 20th-century Europe, and counts among its many treasures Greek sculpture and

112

Roman sarcophagi; medieval ivories and Old Master paintings; Art Nouveau jewellery and 19th-century European and American masterpieces."

Another attraction, which took their interest, was "Historic Ships in Baltimore".

"Historic Ships in Baltimore" is home port to USS Constellation, the last all-sail warship built by the US Navy; the submarine USS Torsk, which sank the last two enemy combatants of WWII; USGC Cutter Taney, the last surviving vessel to witness the Japanese attack on Pearl Harbour, 7 December 1941; Lightship 116 Chesapeake, which marked the entrance to the Chesapeake Bay and the Seven Foot Knoll Lighthouse."

On various weekends they visited the American Visionary Art Museum and the Baltimore Museum of Art.

One weekend they drove the forty miles to Washington D.C to discover the national capital. On another they flew to New York on a long weekend and took in a show on Broadway, "Mowtown the Musical" They both always loved the music and they loved the show. They took the elevator to the top of the Empire State Building and visited "Ground Zero".

All in all, it was a great year. They made new friends and experienced American life but the time had come to return to Sydney, Australia.

Kate was due to present her paper as the final step to qualifying as a Master in Radiology and Steve was due to begin his fourth year at RPA. He had made the decision not to pursue a career in Neurology.

113

Bring in the Human Guinea Pigs

Chapter 20

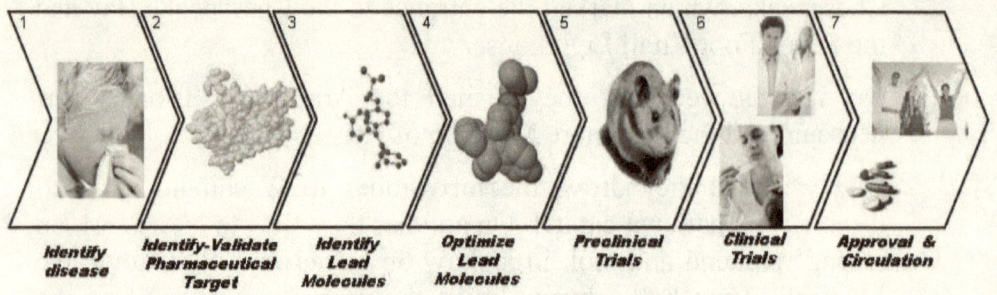

1 Identify disease 2 Identify-Validate Pharmaceutical Target 3 Identify Lead Molecules 4 Optimize Lead Molecules 5 Preclinical Trials 6 Clinical Trials 7 Approval & Circulation

Timeline from Inception to Commercial Release of a New Drug

Rob had begun a presentation to DRC's board; he was determined to take them back to basics so there was no illusion that AS252 would be released any time soon.

Up on the screen he projected the seven stages of drug development.

'Ladies and Gentlemen, we are at stage five and so far we have achieved amazing results in the pre-clinical stage but now we enter the crucial stage of clinical trials. This stage will last six to seven years.'

Clinical Trial Phase Six Years

Patients Participating

Stage 1 twenty to one hundred

Stage 2 One hundred to five hundred

Stage 3 One thousand to five thousand

Approval and Circulation Two Years

TGA Approval

Large Scale Manufacturing

Estimate cost One Billion Dollars

You all need to decide if you are to sign off on Stage Five. If you do, we believe the potential for this Alzheimer's cure will be at least twenty billion dollars, if not more in the life of the patent.

That's not discounting the millions of Alzheimer's sufferers we would be helping.'

The Chairperson of the board spoke.

'My board and I are aware of the risks yet we all feel this is the project for DRC. We will give you and your team the necessary approvals and congratulations to you Rob and your team.'

The meeting ended and everybody dispersed except for Rob and Henry.

'Mate, I couldn't help but think through your presentation of the consequences if we hadn't taken the risk of putting you on the program.

You wouldn't be making the presentation; you may not have been working here. We are now entering Stage Five, knowing full well it works on humans.'

'Don't worry, Henry, the irony wasn't lost on me. Come on, let's go down to the pub and celebrate.'

'Sounds good to me, mate.'

The clinical trials were organised taking about six months to find appropriate patients. Doctors from around the state were also involved in the monitoring of progress. Once stage three was reached, people from around the country would be registered and participating.

The lab mice were also closely monitored as a parallel testing program continued with the furry little patients.

Rob was in his office going over the progress reports of the clinical trial participants. So far they paralleled his own progress at the early stages of his program.

Henry knocked on his office door.

'Come in, mate. Take a seat and look at these reports. It's all looking good.'

Henry sat down but didn't look at the reports; he looked quite glum.

'What's wrong with you, mate, did your dog die?'

'I'm afraid I've got some disturbing news, Rob.'

'Well, what is it? Come on, out with it.'

'The mice have begun to regress. I've been watching them over the past month. I thought it was an anomaly.'

'What do you mean, a fucking anomaly?'

'It was only a couple. The rest seemed normal but now it seems all of them are back to full Alzheimer's'

'Shit! I don't fucking believe it. This has got to be a bad dream.'

'No, mate, it's real.'

116

'Well just because the mice have regressed doesn't mean I'll follow. Mice and men are different.'

'You may be right but I doubt it.'

'Yeah I know I'm clutching at straws. Maybe I need to be on a continuing dose; plenty of other medicines are prescribed for life.'

'I thought of that. We could give it a try.'

'I don't have time do I?'

'Not really.'

'Let me think about it.'

'Let's talk again tomorrow'

'OK, mate. Try and sleep tonight. Are you going to tell Andy?'

'I don't know.'

The following morning Rob got to the lab an hour late, a very unusual occurrence; he went straight to Henry's office and shut the door.

'G'day, mate, how are you feeling? Did you sleep?'

'I didn't get much but I did come up with a plan.'

'Well, what have you come up with?'

'We know that AL252 has been successful in curing the disease albeit on a temporary basis.'

'True.'

'We also know this has been achieved by the team working out how an enzyme triggers the destruction of neurons in the brain. Despite the apparent failure, we have obtained extraordinary knowledge about how the enzyme gamma secretase can be modulated. If we tell the board about the problem, clinical trials of the drug may have to be abandoned. We know our own program and those of our competitors have been trying to target gamma secretase to treat Alzheimer's for over a decade. Our work suggests that molecules we discovered modulate rather than inhibit the enzyme. We

117

believed this would offer a cure with no or very few side effects.'

'Rob, you're not telling me anything new. How is this going to overcome the problem?'

'If we can determine why AS252 initially inhibits the enzyme then reverses the process we will have solved the problem.'

'Easier said than done, mate. If we have to conduct this research clandestinely with no real resources, we will be pushing it up hill.'

'Well, this is the other part of the plan. I propose I go to the board and spill the beans. They have two choices, they kick me out on my arse and my career is effectively over or they back the new research with money and people, which could effectively protect their huge investment.'

'You forget my career would also be over.'

'Not at all, I won't tell them about your involvement I will take full responsibility.'

'What about your Mum's program?'

'I am not going to mention it. No need.'

'Well mate, we don't have too many options do we? I think you're right. We need to tell the board and see what happens.'

A Race Against Time

Chapter 21

Rob walked into the boardroom of DRC fully accepting that he could be leaving the room unemployed with his research reputation in tatters.

The chairperson opened the meeting.

'Fellow board members, Dr Iffinger has requested this extraordinary meeting to bring us up to date with recent developments of which he feels we should all be made aware. Dr Iffinger has not briefed me on the subject matter so I am as much in the dark as you. Rob, the floor is yours.'

'Thank you, Margaret, there have been some disturbing developments in the development of AS252.'

Rob went on to explain his condition and the illegal trial and the initial results.

Initially the reaction of the board was favourable; even though the trial by Rob was illegal, they had empathy for his situation. They also seemed pleased that he had been cured, ratifying their faith in the drug. It was only when he went on to describe current developments with the laboratory mice that things became tense.

He put forward his development scheme and left it with the board to make their decision.

'Rob, we'll discuss the options open to us and get back to you in a week. In the meantime, you are under suspension and are not permitted to enter DRC's premises. Do you understand?'

'Yes, Madam Chair, I fully understand.'

Rob left the boardroom with mixed feelings. They could have dismissed him instantly and that would be that. The fact they were taking a week to make their decision could be a good thing. His next problem was to explain to Andy why he had a week off at such short notice.

The meeting closed at 3pm he decided to go straight home and decide what he would do while on suspension. Andy arrived home at his usual time of 5.30pm, walked into the apartment and was surprised to see Rob watching television and eating cashews out of a bowl with a scotch next to him.

'Well, look at you, what are you doing home so early? Get the sack?

'Almost; I'm suspended for a week.'

Rob had decided to tell Andy everything including his likely regression back into Alzheimer's. Andy was horrified and began to cry. He couldn't be consoled.

'I can't fucking believe it. There's no justice in this world... just when I thought we had had a future, this Alzheimer's bitch comes back and bites us on the bum.'

'Mate, we still have a future. I'm determined to find the cause of the drug's failure, I promise you.'

'You may even not have a fucking job, Rob, how are you going to fix it? In the fucking kitchen?'

'Andy, let's not worry about whether I have a job or access to the lab until the board comes back with an answer. They've got a lot to lose if they decide to pack up and walk away. I'm talking billions.'

The two partners had a very sombre night, going to bed early. Next morning Andy seemed to be more optimistic. He decided he would call the pharmacy and ask for the week off: his request was granted.

They tried not to discuss their situation and spent the week going to the movies and shopping for clothes and furnishing items.

On the Friday Rob received a call from Margaret, the Chairperson of the Board. She informed him that he was expected back in the lab on Monday and the unanimous decision was that he should stay and try and resolve the drug's issues. There were provisos, including secrecy.

120

Rob got off the telephone and let out a loud YES. Andy came running in and hugged his soul- mate.

'I take it you kept you job, mate?'

'Yep, that's fantastic! At least I can try and fix the problem, not only for me but millions of sufferers around the world.'

'This deserves a celebration. I'm booking the "Rock Pool' tonight.'

'Do it.'

Rob arrived at the lab at the normal time on Monday morning and immediately went to Henry's office; naturally he was delighted that Rob was back and ready to get to work.

'Did you have any thoughts on where the problem lies, mate?'

'I think it has to do with the misfolded proteins regenerating after being initially suppressed by AS252. For some reason we have been able to minimise its production but it regained its strength, stopping the essential proteins being produced. As you know, without these proteins, the brain cells die off.'

'Yeah but we thought we had nailed it with the drug. Now we're back to square one.'

'Not necessarily. I think we almost had it but there is just one piece of the jigsaw that we missed. That's what we need to be working on, not starting all over again.'

'It sounds like a logical approach; let's get on with it.'

Rob called the team together and briefed them on the problem and assigned them each a specific task. Rob and Henry were working twelve-hour days, six days a week. Some in the team followed their example. Rob knew they were working against the clock, his clock.

Looking Good

Chapter 22

John was beginning to see real changes in Bev's behaviour; she had been on the AS252 program for three months. She still hated her weekly injection but quietly accepted it without abusing poor Henry.

She had begun to dress herself choosing appropriate and tasteful clothing; she also could retain some of what she read in newspapers and magazines, even commenting on some of the stories. Although she still enjoyed her wine, John no longer had to hide the bottle; she knew when she had had enough.

Before starting the program, it was agreed by John that Rob and Henry would assess her progress by giving Bev the retina test and the normal Alzheimer's assessment.

The day to visit DRC had arrived and John and Bev took the ferry across the harbour and walked from Circular Quay, the same route Rob took every workday morning.

Henry greeted them in reception and took them into his office. He explained the procedure and began the series of tests.

He asked John and Bev to wander down to the Arabic café for a coffee while he processed the results. An hour later they returned. Henry brought them back into his office and gave them the news.

> 'Bev, when you started on the program you were assessed as stage five. Your results today indicate you are now stage three. Based on these results, there is no reason not to believe in another three months you will be cured.'

> 'Are you absolutely sure, Henry?' asked John.

> 'You can never be absolutely sure but I'm very confident.'

> John squeezed his wife's hand and kissed her on the cheek.

'Thank you, Henry, we really appreciate what you've done for us.'

'John, it's not over yet but you can start to enjoy life a bit more.'

The elated couple left the building and returned via ferry to their apartment.

When John walked into their beautiful home he thanked his lucky stars he hadn't sold it. It had been viewed by a couple of agents who were very keen to list it. He had even begun looking for suitable houses in the Blue Mountains so he could be close to the proposed nursing home.

Henry and Rob had agreed they would keep Bev on the program and not inform John of the problems. Rob felt that even if his mother regressed back to where she was before starting the drug, it would give his parents some quality time together.

By the fifth month Bev was almost back to normal. She and John were happy and enjoying their life together. They could now go to the theatre with the confidence that she wouldn't yell out "bullshit" if she didn't like the performance. They had spent a couple of weekends away and it was like old times.

Rob had suggested that his mother tackle some simple crosswords to begin exercising her brain. She used to do "The Australian" cryptic every day during her morning tea at the law practice and her staff were amazed how quickly she solved them.

Bev also began to remember her time as a lawyer and could recall some of her more critical cases. John promised himself that when she was completely cured, they would take a trip to Canada and the United States, two places Bev had never been.

Things were really getting much better.

Rob and the team were working at a frantic pace; there had to be a solution in negating PERK, the enzyme that was instrumental in activating the defence mechanism thus stopping the necessary proteins from restoring normal brain behaviour.

Time was running out for Rob. He knew if they didn't make a breakthrough soon, he would resort to full on Alzheimer's and eventually end up in a nursing home with no or little understanding what was going on around him.

He was due to pick up Steve and Kate at the airport on Friday morning. Steve and Kate had terminated their apartment leases when they left for America, so Rob had found them a new one close to McMahons point. This was to be a new beginning as Mr and Mrs Iffinger.

The plane was two hours late but fortunately Rob had the "Flightradar24" app on his phone which enabled him to track their flight from take-off in New York to landing in Sydney. He arrived right on time. Steve and Kate walked out to see Rob standing there with a huge grin on his face.

'Hi you guys. How are the weary travellers?'

'G'day Rob, good to see you, mate.'

'Hi Rob.' Kate put her arms around him and kissed him on the cheek.

'Well, we better get this show on the road. Can I help you with your bags?'

'Sure, why not? They're on wheels so it's not too bad.'

They found Rob's car eventually. He thought it was on level two but in fact it was on level five.

They arrived at the new apartment; both Steve and Kate were awestruck.

'This place is amazing, Rob. I can't believe you found it. Look at those city views.'

'You've done well, Rob. Thanks, bro.'

'I'm glad you like it, guys. It's not easy to find a two bedroom in this area for the rent you'll be paying.'

'You're right there; the rent is great, much cheaper than I thought we'd have to pay.'

Unbeknown to Steve and Kate, Rob had negotiated with the agent to pay half the rent to help out the couple. The agent was under strict instructions not to divulge the fact to them.

'OK, time I went. I have to go back to the lab. Why don't we get together with Andy tomorrow night?'

'Sounds great. Where?'

'Come over to our place at about 6.30pm.'

'We'll be there. By that time, we might be feeling a bit better. In the meantime, we're going to bed. I don't care what they say about staying up and body clocks etc.'

'Right, we'll see you then.'

The next night Steve and Kate walked the one kilometre to Rob and Andy's apartment. They both agreed it was better than driving and trying to find a park, which was almost impossible.

They rang the bell, Andy opened the door, greeting them both enthusiastically.

'Hello, hello, how are the yanks?'

'Hi, Andy. We're not bloody yanks, God help us.'

'Come in, can I get you a drink?'

'I'll have a white wine, thanks Andy.'

'What about you, Steve?'

'I think I'll have a beer if you have one, please.'

'Of course we have one, name your poison.'

'Would you have a Boags? I haven't tasted the Tasmanian nectar for over a year.'

'My favourite too. One Boags coming up.'

'Rob, what can I get you?' Andy yelled.

'Scotch please.' Rob came out of the kitchen and greeted them both.

'Hi, guys, how'd you sleep?'

'Like a pair of babies, mate.'

'Good, come out to the balcony while Andy fixes our drinks.

So, tell us all about it.'

'Hey, wait till I'm out there. I don't want to miss anything,' yelled Andy from the kitchen.

Andy brought a tray of drinks out and passed them around.

'Right then. From the start, if you don't mind,' instructed Rob.

'OK, well we got on the plane and sat down in our allocated seats.'

'Alright, smart arse, from the time you landed in America will do.'

'Sorry, Rob, but you did say from the start.'

'You always were a sarcastic little bugger.'

'All right, well, as you know we had a week in San Francisco to acclimatise ourselves to the American way of life. It was fantastic wasn't it, Kate?

'Absolutely wonderful! I'm more than ready to go back.'

'We did the usual tourist thing, went on a tour of Alcatraz, saw the giant redwoods etc.

We flew to Maryland where John Hopkins put us up in a very nice hotel until we moved into our hospital apartment.'

'What was the apartment like, mate?'

'Not as nice as our new one here but it was fine, a little cramped but we enjoyed staying there. It was close to restaurants and shops so we tended to walk everywhere.'

'You weren't concerned about being mugged?' asked Andy.

'No, not at all, we felt very safe.'

'Did you see any other parts of the country, mate?'

'We drove to Washington a couple of times, visiting the usual sites like the White House and The Lincoln Museum. I think we both agree New York was the highlight,' Steve said.

'I've always wanted to go to New York. What's it really like?' asked Rob.

'Once you've been there, you can understand why they call it "The Big Apple". You can't really describe it because there's no other city in the world like it. We couldn't believe the number of high rises; just one street has more than the whole of Sydney!'

'Did you go to Broadway?' asked Andy.

'Sure did. We saw a new show called "Mowtown the Musical". The music was unbelievable! People were jumping up and dancing in the aisles.'

'Mate, you and I are going. We can get a round-the-world ticket,' said Rob.

The four of them sat at the dining table and Rob served his pièce de résistance, coq au vin.

'Rob, I had no idea you were such a good cook,' Kate enthused.

'Don't compliment him too much, Kate, he'll get a big head.'

'Come on, Andy, we all know you are the resident chef. There's only one dish I can cook and this is it, so enjoy.'

'Have you contacted Mum and Dad since you've been back, Steve?'

'Yeah I rang this morning and they both sound really good. I was surprised how 'with it' Mum was.'

'Did you call them much when you were over in the States, mate?'

'We did, we Skyped once a week but Mum still seemed pretty vague. This morning she was happy and wanted to speak to us both which was unusual.'

'I think the Alzheimer's is actually regressing. We have tried some new treatments and it seems to be helping.'

'That's incredible, mate. I must say I've never heard of Alzheimer's regressing, no matter what the treatment.'

'It may not last forever but in the meantime, let's enjoy her company,' Rob advised.

The remainder of the evening was spent eating, drinking and laughing.

Steve was due to start back at RPA the following Monday, as was Kate, so they used the few days they had left, buying furnishings and moving their existing goods and chattels out of storage and into their apartment.

Blue Haven

Chapter 23

Dr James Russell had wanted to be a doctor since the age of ten; he knew helping people was his calling. He grew up in the affluent Eastern suburb of Woollahra in Sydney with his sister, Leonie. His father and mother were both doctors so it could be said 'medicine' was in his genes.

Young Jim was an A Grade student as was Leonie; they both passed their Higher School Certificate in the top one per cent. Jim enrolled in medicine at the University of New South Wales; Leonie enrolled in the same university, doing law.

Before beginning his medical degree, Jim was given the opportunity to work in a nursing home in the Blue Mountains. He took the opportunity, as aged care was where his interest lay. He was to work at Blue Haven during the summer break, four weeks in all.

His first day entailed helping patients to the dining room,

cleaning the floors and alike; it was not a very interesting start.

He observed that many of the dementia patients were spaced out, not knowing what was going on around them. He asked a nurse he had befriended why this was so.

'Many of them are either aggressive or obnoxious and difficult to handle. We find the best way to manage them is dose them up with antipsychotic drugs like olanzapine. Once they kick in, the patients are like little lambs.'

Jim was not yet a doctor but he knew this was wrong. Surely there were other means that could be employed more conducive to proper care.

Over the four weeks, Jim became more and more convinced that elderly patients were being treated badly. Doctors were more than happy to prescribe drugs that would make it easier for nursing home staff to manage those under their care.

The whole system was wrong. Dementia patients require special skills. He decided that when he qualified and completed his internship he would specialise in dementia and elderly care.

James, as he now preferred to be called, graduated at the top of his year and was eagerly sought by a number of hospitals. He chose Prince Henry's in Randwick not far from where he lived; he chose this hospital because it had a reputation for treating dementia patients.

He spent his internship learning about dementia and how patients should be cared for.

At the end of the year, he applied for and was accepted as resident physician at Blue Haven Nursing Home. He was determined to make this aged facility the best in the state.

James arrived at Blue Haven on his first day, full of hope and enthusiasm; he was welcomed by the General Manager, Ms Dianne Walsh, who had been at Blue Haven for over fifteen years.

'Welcome to Blue Haven, Doctor Russell, I am sure you would like me to show you around.'

'Thank you, Ms Walsh, but may I ask a few questions first?'

'Please call me Di; why yes of course. What would you like to know?'

'How many dementia patients are currently housed here?'

'Fifty.'

'How many would fall into the category "hard to handle"?'

'None, they are all under control, God bless them.'

'OK, how many are being prescribed anti-psychotic medication?'

'I don't know, James. I suppose most of them.'

'Why?'

'You know as well as I do that if we don't medicate them, this place becomes a mad house, bedlam.'

'What I do know is that with proper treatment and diligent caring, most of your patients will not need drugs.'

'So, it is your intention to barge in here and change everything? Things run smoothly, James, don't fuck it up.'

'As you are aware, the board has appointed me as resident physician. You would also know that this is the first time a resident has been appointed. I have sole responsibility for prescribing drugs, any drugs. No longer will local doctors come in here and prescribe whatever the nursing staff request. Each patient will be individually assessed after they have ceased their antipsychotic medication. Once they have been assessed, a decision on treatment will be made.'

'I see, so you become God. You decide who needs what and when they need it without consultation.'

'No, I don't decide without consultation. Two other doctors will be involved. Dr Steven Iffinger, a highly regarded clinician, and Dr Marusha Belenko, a psychiatrist who specialises in dementia care.

Now, I would like to be shown the facility, Di, thank you'.

Di led the way, showing James the kitchen and dining room; although it was only ten am, the tables had been set for lunch.

'What time do the residents have lunch, Di?'

'Eleven. It suits our kitchen staff to feed them early. I can assure you that the residents, as you call them, are more than happy to eat at that time.'

'I'm sure they are. They have no choice,' he thought to himself.'

'The most popular room in the home is the TV room. Our patients, sorry, residents, sit here for hours watching Andre Rieu or Dad's Army or a movie of some sort.'

'What's the favourite movie?'

'*Oklahoma* is the pick.'

131

'Do you have any other activities available?'

'We tried a couple of activities although none of the residents seemed interested. Their attention span is very poor.'

'I have found that in dealing with Alzheimer's/Dementia patients, you need to try to find out what your residents like and their individual needs, read their history, talk to their families, ask them. You will find that different activities will work some days and times and others won't.

The best thing to remember is that the residents are not babies and should be treated with respect at all times. Have fun with them and keep them busy, look out for 'sundowning' (restless behaviour towards the late afternoon hours). Try to keep a consistent program. Enjoy yourself!'

'I see, so what do you suggest, James?'

'When I did my internship at Prince Henry's they engaged their residents in a range of activities. The residents loved it, as did the nursing staff. Some examples were:

Sorting
Get items that can be sorted by the residents such as buttons (different sizes and colours), poker chips, balls, bottle caps, forks, spoons, rocks, etc. Have residents' sort items out; make sure to always have staff by the resident to watch that they don't eat items.

Play Dough
Give resident some clay or play dough and have them make something, anything. This is good exercise for their hands.

Book Making
Have your residents go through different magazines and look for a specific item. Examples: birds, ladies, babies, cats, dogs, food, cars etc., then have residents cut the items out and make their own "books."

What's in the Bag?
Get a bag and fill it with different items such as cotton balls, sandpaper, leaves, newspaper, felt, -tips, golf balls, socks, clothes peg, etc., then have residents take turns and feel what's in the bag, and tell you what the items are.

Stringing
Get cheerios, fruit loops, popcorn, or honey smacks cereal and some string and let your residents string up a chain to put outside for the birds. This activity is fun because they can eat some while they make their chains. They also love watching the birds eat them.

Cooking Class
Make a fruit salad: get different fruits and have residents cut it up with plastic knives, add whipped cream or plain yoghurt. They'll love it.

Other stuff to make:
Tuna Salad, Smoothies, Ice cream Sundaes, Pizza Boats, and Nachos. You'll find they will begin to remember the dishes they used to make in their own kitchens.

Pet Therapy
Having animals living in the facility can be a lot of work but the residents really respond to dogs, cats, rabbits, birds, turtles etc. And the fun part is that you can get your residents to help with their care, feeding, and walking the dogs.

Life Skills
Have residents fold clothes, sweep, dust, vacuum and set dining room tables. Alzheimer's residents love to help. I have found that if you say" I am so busy, can you help me fold these clothes, Mrs Johnson?" they will love to do it.'

'James, how do you expect my staff to organise all these extra activities? They would have no time left to conduct their normal duties.'

133

'Like giving them knock out pills twice a day?' he thought.

'Don't dismiss these ideas, Di. You may well find your job and that of your staff members would actually become easier.'

'I doubt it.'

The two of them moved on to inspect the residents' rooms; some had their own personal TV and plenty of photos and pictures on the walls. They were quite comfortable. Others had nothing… no TV, no photos, nothing to remind them of home. These rooms reminded James of prison cells.

'Why is there such a disparity between rooms, Di?'

'You mean some have photos and a TV and others nothing?'

'Yeah, why is that?'

'The relatives and friends of the residents bring in all the home comforts. The others either have no living relatives or if they do, they just don't care.'

'That's sad, very sad.'

'Yes it is.'

'Have you approached any of the charities like the Salvation Army to see if they could help?'

'No, I hadn't thought of it.'

'It might be worth a try, I mean they couldn't help with photos but they may be able to help with pictures or a TV or throw- overs, things like that.'

'OK, I'll try contacting them.'

'If you like I can do it as I know you have a lot on your plate.'

'If you wish.'

Steve knew that had he left it to Di, nothing would be done. His father knew someone who was very senior in the Salvos so he would try and elicit his support.

Next stop was the TV lounge where there were about twenty recliners in the room, all occupied by residents. Di was right in saying this was the favourite room in the house.

Most of the residents were asleep but the few who were awake seemed in a hypnotic trance as Curly McLean sang "Oh What a Beautiful Mornin".

'So I take it most of these people are heavily medicated?'

'Yes I suppose they are, but if they weren't, they would all be causing mischief.'

'What do you mean, 'mischief'?'

'Well, take Mr Brown over there. He owned a furniture removal company, a quite successful one I'm told.

When he was living at home, his wife would awaken countless times to find him emptying the lounge, hauling heavy bits of furniture out onto the front lawn in the middle of the night. On one occasion Mrs Brown left him for a few hours to go shopping and she returned to find the entire downstairs had been cleared, including the washing machine and dryer.

He pulled a glass cabinet off the wall and it smashed down on him, badly lacerating his arms and face. That was the last straw. Mrs Brown approached us and we admitted him.'

'So, how was he while here?'

'We had similar problems. Furniture was moved around and residents often found furniture in their rooms that did not belong there. The only way to stop him was to prescribe olanzapine to quieten him down. Now look at him; he's sitting quietly watching his favourite movie.'

'OK, Di, let's go back to your office and talk about what we can do to improve these people's quality of life.'

'I don't see what you can do. They're all very happy and content.'

'Let's go to your office.'

In Search of Excellence
And
Incompetence

Chapter 24

Di and James entered the General Manager's office and sat down in the visitors' chairs.

'Would you like me to ask Sally to bring us some coffee, James?'

'Yes, that would be nice, thank you.'

'So, what is your grand plan to improve Blue Haven?'

'No grand plan, Di, but I believe there needs to be some changes. As I intimated earlier, there will be an assessment of each resident's condition and the need for medication. If we can cease medication for some of the residents, we have achieved our goal.'

'Your goal.'

'It should be yours as well, Di.'

Sally brought in the coffee and biscuits and placed them on the coffee table.

'I'm not proposing we take everybody off their medication at the same time, Di, I think four at a time will be manageable for everyone. Once the assessments have been completed, the committee of three will make their decision.'

'So how do you propose to choose your first batch?'

'Hardly a batch I would have thought. The first one I would choose is Mr Brown; his condition will be easily

136

assessed. If he starts moving furniture around again we know we've got a problem.

As for the other three, Marusha and Steve will be here tomorrow to assess the residents and interview nursing staff. After that process is complete, we will choose.'

'Well, I look forward to meeting them both.'

'Yeah, sure,' James thought.

Marusha had been born in Sydney to Ukrainian immigrants who had escaped the harsh conditions in Ukraine after the war.

She had heard her parents' stories of life during and after the Second World War in the Ukraine and was thankful her parents immigrated to Australia. She had enjoyed a wonderful life in 'the lucky country', but by no means easy. Her family struggled to eke out a living, yet Marusha was able to attend Sydney University and obtain a degree in Psychology. After several years working in the private sector, she decided to specialise in assessing and working with dementia patients.

Steve and Marusha arrived at Blue Haven at nine am, hoping the residents had finished their breakfast. They had.

The three dedicated professionals assessed Mr Brown first; he was quiet and spoke little. It was obvious to the three that he was on a high dose of olanzapine. The plan was to take him off the drug and reassess in a fortnight. It would be that assessment which would determine the future course of action.

This same plan of action would apply to the other three residents they had chosen to be included in phase one of assessments.

Mrs Marjorie Jones, Mr Stan Nye and Mr Frank Nugent were the other residents assessed that day. They were all removed from their medication and would be assessed in two weeks.

James, being the resident, would monitor their behaviour on a daily basis and include his observations in a report, which would be presented to the assessment group when they met next.

Marusha visited Blue Haven twice a week and she observed changes in behaviour for all four but it was Mr Brown who gained her interest. He had gone back to his old removalist ways, moving small pieces of furniture around the place but no big items yet. Di was complaining and suggesting that she was right: residents had to be dosed up to be manageable.

One Friday, James looked in on the television room and was surprised to see Mr Brown quite relaxed, talking to a nurse with a cup of tea in his hand. Once he finished his tea, he began to rise from the recliner when the nurse spoke.

'Mr Brown, it will be your tea break in fifteen minutes so you may as well stay till then.'

He smiled, nodded his head and sat down again.

James was amazed; he started to walk back to his office when he bumped into Marusha.

'Marusha, you'll never guess what I just saw in the TV room. Mr Brown was drinking tea, relaxed as a cat in an easy chair.'

'I think you'll find me responsible for that, James.'

'What do you mean?'

'I was thinking about when I moved recently; I could see the removalists worked bloody hard so when they had their tea break they sat down, opened their thermoses, poured themselves a nice cup of tea and chatted amongst themselves. They really relished that tea break. I thought this could be worth trying on Mr Brown and it worked. He's on a perpetual tea break.'

'Well done! Great psychology, Marusha. How are you going with the others?'

'Not as well as with Mr Brown but I think I'm making headway. I'll bring you up to date at the end of the day.'

'OK, see you at five for drinks.'

Although it was only the end of the first week James felt confident that the path he was proposing was the right one. He looked forward to having a drink with his two partners, Marusha and Steve, at the end of the day and getting their opinions.

Five o'clock came and Steve walked into James's office. Marusha was yet to arrive when the clock passed five thirty, James and Steve decided they should go looking for her. She wasn't in the TV room or the dining room; they looked outside in the gardens but couldn't find their colleague.

Steve suggested they check the rooms of the residents participating in the trial. They looked in on Marjorie who was lying on her bed watching "Millionaire Hot Seat". They were both pleased she was so calm; although she had no idea what the show was about, she enjoyed the colour and excitement. They then tried Stan. His door was locked and there were muffled sounds coming from inside. James used his skeleton key to open the door. The two doctors were horrified, Marusha was gagged and bound on the bed, Stan stood beside her with a kitchen knife in his hand, threatening to 'slit the bitch's throat.'

> 'Stan, please give me the knife, then we can talk about what's upset you so much.'

> 'Fuck off! You're just as bad as she is.'

> 'Why do you think that, mate?'

> 'I'm not your fucking mate, now get out.'

> 'OK, I'll leave but can Steve stay?'

> 'Who's he?'

> 'He's a good bloke who wants to help you.'

> 'OK, he can stay but you can fuck off.'

> 'OK, I'm going.'

James left the room and ran to his office, calling 000 as he went. He explained the situation to the operator who put him through to the Leura Police Station, only five minutes away.

The police arrived without sirens ten minutes later. They didn't want to warn Stan of their presence.

They first spoke to James about the situation and the lay-out of the room. Stan was standing with his back to a large picture window; the police were hoping they could surprise him. After discussion, they decided against that tactic. The decision was made to open the door and fire a Taser gun at Stan, hopefully immobilizing him.

The police sergeant, George Riddle, flung open the door to find Stan holding the knife over Murusha's throat,with Steve tied up in the corner. He fired several times and finally Stan dropped to the floor writhing around in pain. Three more police ran in and handcuffed him they then untied Marusha and Steve and got them out of the there.

Stan was sedated and put into a safe room where he would stay until a decision was made as to what to do with him.

Marusha was driven by ambulance to the Leura Private Hospital for examination; fortunately she had not been harmed physically but was terribly shaken up by her ordeal. Steve, who had accompanied her in the ambulance, recommended she take a week off and prescribed some mild sedatives.

He returned to Blue Haven and asked for a meeting with James and Di to try to determine what triggered the violent episode with Mr Nye.

They decided not to question Marusha until she returned from her sick leave.

'Have you got any idea, Di, what caused this violent outburst from Stan?'

'Not really, James, he has lashed out a couple of times at staff when they were helping him shower or go to the toilet but nothing like what we just witnessed.'

'Have you noticed any change in mood?'

'No, although he has suffered depression years ago before he was diagnosed with Alzheimer's.'

'Why isn't that recorded in his file?'

'It was only his wife mentioning it one day that I became aware of it.'

'Anything like that should be recorded as it is likely that Stan is suffering depression right now. Depression is a common trigger for violence; if the team had known, we would not have taken him off his medication.'

'Stan needs a complete reassessment and he needs the relevant prescribed drugs.'

'You won't be asking the police to press charges?'

No, although Marusha has the final say.'

'Steve, what's your view?'

'I agree with everything you've said, James. We can't blame Stan for his actions. He had no control, but having said that, there is no doubt he needs to be medicated and taken off the trial.'

'OK, I'll prescribe some medication with Steve's consultation and we need to move him into a room that can't be locked from the inside.'

'Speaking of locks, how many residents have doors lockable from the inside?' asked Steve.

'They all do; it's never been a problem before,' Di said defensively.

'I am going to recommend to the board that all the locks be changed,' said James.

Well it's been a hell of a day. I suggest we all go home and have a drink.'

'I'm with you, James.' Said Steve.

Stan was medicated and had no recollection of the event but he was treated for his depression and although drugged, was not a zombie and interacted well with the staff and other residents.

You Never Know What's Around the Corner

Chapter 25

Kate had been born into a privileged family; her father, Roger, had begun an electrical goods store soon after he married Kate's mother, Jan. Through hard work and diligence they had built the business to the point where they owned and operated thirty stores in three states, New South Wales, Victoria and Queensland. Combined income for the group was approaching one hundred million dollars when a still larger group offered fifty million dollars for the business and five million in stock.

Roger was fifty-eight, Jan was fifty-five; they still had plenty of energy and their health was good. They had not thought about selling the business but it was difficult not to accept the offer. After extensive discussion they decided to accept. Under the terms of the contract Roger and Jan were precluded from opening a store or stores in opposition for five years.

The first thing they did after handing the keys over was to go on a first class trip around the world. It had always been their ambition to travel extensively but the business restricted how long they could be away.

After twelve months of travel they were happy to be back home in Sydney. Kate and Steve met them at the airport and drove them home to their beautiful home in Mosman.

Roger began playing golf three times a week and managed to cut five strokes off his handicap. Jan became actively involved in a number of charities including "Beyond Blue" an organisation that supported people with mental conditions such as depression.

Overall, life was good but then Roger found a small brown mole on his left foot while he was drying off after shower at the golf club.

One of his mates in his regular foursome was a well renowned skin cancer specialist.

'Frank, do you mind having a look at this? I'm sure it's nothing but you never know.'

'Sure, Rog, where is it, mate?'

'Just here under my foot.'

'OK, let me see. It's hard to tell but I don't think we should risk it, mate. I think you'd better come down and see me at the surgery first thing Monday morning where I can conduct some tests.'

'Sure, you don't think it's a melanoma do you?'

'I don't know, Roger, not until I can conduct a detailed examination.'

Roger went home deciding not to mention it to Jan. After all, he thought it was probably nothing - just a big freckle.

He tried not to think about it over the weekend. They had some good friends over on the Sunday for a BBQ; everybody had a very pleasant afternoon.

Roger slept well, waking at his usual time of six am, as did Jan. Their weekday routine was to walk down to the harbour shore and then climb the steep hill back up to the house about two kilometres in all. Roger felt no pain in his left foot, which was reassuring.

He had agreed to be at Frank's surgery at nine thirty. He made the excuse that he needed to visit the hardware store for a few odds and ends.

Roger arrived at Dr Picard's surgery right on time; he wasn't kept waiting long. The mole was examined under a bright light, whereupon Frank decided it should be removed and clinically tested.

This was done under a local anaesthetic and then sent to the lab.

'We should get the results back in a couple of days, mate. We'll call you when we know the result. Don't worry, I'm sure it will be fine.'

'Thanks, Frank, I appreciate it.'

'Don't mention it. I 'll send you a bill when this is all over.'

'I'm sure you will.'

The following Thursday Roger received a telephone call from Frank. He was advised that he should come into the surgery that afternoon to discuss the results. Frank refused to elaborate until he saw Roger in person.

Roger was ushered into his good friend's office upon arrival.

'Take a seat, mate. We have received the results back and I'm afraid the news isn't very good.'

'What do you mean?'

'I'm afraid you have a melanoma.'

'Oh shit.'

'Not all melanomas are a death sentence, Roger. There are plenty of examples where they have been cured. It just takes a bit of work.'

'I read on the web that it depends how soon the melanoma is detected and treated. I've got no idea how long it's been there. I don't normally examine the soles of my feet, for God's sake.'

'Let's think positively. First thing is we need to operate to ensure all the cancer has been removed. I need to examine the lymph nodes to ensure the cancer hasn't metastasised there.'

'Can you run by me exactly what you are going to do, Frank? I'd like to know.'

As you know, Roger, you have been diagnosed with melanoma after the biopsy of a skin lesion came back positive. It is my intention to remove more skin around the area of melanoma. We will make a wide local excision around an area of skin and tissue surrounding the melanoma and remove it.

Once I've removed the skin and tissue I will extend down to your muscle, but none of your muscle will be removed. The amount of tissue removed around the melanoma depends on what we call the Breslow depth of the melanoma.

144

I estimate that one to two centimetres of skin and tissue will be removed surrounding the melanoma. This additional skin and tissue is removed to help prevent a recurrence of the melanoma. There is a high chance that the melanoma will recur on your foot if this additional skin and tissue is not removed.

Depending on how the surgery goes, we should be able to get away with not performing a skin graft. We'll just use a flap of skin to close it up.'

'It all sounds straightforward, mate. How long do you think I'll be off the golf course?'

'I would think three weeks and you'll be back beating the crap out of me again.'

Roger's surgery was booked in for the following Monday at RPA. Steve had requested he assist and his request was granted.

When Dr Picard examined the lymph nodes, he looked up at Steve and explained he would need to remove all the glands near his foot and that meant up to the groin. Steve acknowledged this and the fairly simple operation thus became much more complex.

The patient was brought into intensive care where he remained for three days then transferred to a private room.

Jan spent much of the day and half of the evening sitting with him. Steve and Kate visited everyday and he seemed to be in good spirits chatting about the football results and how he could hardly wait to get back on the golf course.

He had had an MRI on his fifth day in hospital but hadn't heard the results yet. Frank entered the room and approached Roger with a grim face and delivered the news.

'Well, my old mate, the news is not so good.'

'What do you mean, Frank?'

'The MRI has shown up that the cancer has metastasised into the lungs and the brain.'

'Oh shit, more surgery.'

'I'm afraid not, mate. Both tumours are inoperable.'

'So what happens now?'

'We can put you on a massive course of chemotherapy to try and reduce the size of the tumours. We could also try radiation.'

'You don't sound particularly hopeful, Frank.'

'Miracles do occur, Rog, but not too often. The best you can hope for is six months with the treatment, one month without.'

'Come on, Frank, don't beat around the bush!'

'I know you well, mate. I think it's better to know the facts and plan around them.'

'Yeah, you're right. Can you let me talk to Jan and Kate? I'll let you know my decision tomorrow. I can't fucking believe this. I shot an eighty-one on Saturday and I'm on my deathbed on Friday; it just doesn't make sense. I'm not particularly scared of dying but I'm pretty pissed off about cutting my life short. I think I deserve better.'

'That you do, mate.'

Roger was discharged from hospital that day.

He went home and poured himself a large scotch; despite the hour, he needed a drink. He sat down in his favourite chair and contemplated his life thus far. He had a beautiful supportive wife and a successful intelligent daughter. His business life had been an incredible success and he had more money than he knew what to do with; what he didn't have was long to live.

He decided he would tell Jan over dinner and then invite Kate and Steve over for dinner the following night.

Jan returned from a 'Beyond Blue' meeting at about five pm. She sensed something was wrong as soon as she entered the apartment.

'Hello, darling, how did you go with Frank?'

'I'll tell you over dinner, hon.'

'No you bloody won't! You can make me a drink. You've obviously already had one, then you can tell me what's going on.

'OK, you win…as usual.'

Roger poured his wife of thirty years a glass of white wine and they went out to the front veranda.

'I'm afraid the news is not very good, babe. The melanoma has metastasised into my right lung and my brain.'

Jan just looked at her husband. She felt like she was on a different plane. Roger's words were like an echo in the distance. Then a tear fell down her cheek.

'So, when are they going to operate?' she asked, fighting back her tears.

'Both tumours are inoperable I'm afraid.'

'Oh God, so what happens now?'

'They can give me chemotherapy and radiation to try to shrink them.'

'Will that cure you, darling?'

'No, it will extend my life.'

'How long?' She didn't really want to hear the answer.

'Frank seems to think it would give me another six months.'

'Six months? No! This can't be happening. Not to us. What if you don't agree to the treatment?'

'I'll have four to six weeks.'

'I feel ill.'

Jan approached her husband with tears streaming down her face. She hugged him; she couldn't let him go.

'I love you so much, Roger. I won't let you die on me. I won't!'

'Sorry, babe.'

The following night when Kate and Steve came over for dinner, Kate displayed the same reaction: disbelief and grief.

Roger and Jan decided he should embark on a chemotherapy program; he began it the following week.

Roger demonstrated great strength and tenacity but after five months he passed away, leaving his wife and family devastated.

Roger's funeral was held in St Mary's Cathedral with five hundred friends, family and business associates attending.

Jan found life difficult without her husband. He had been her friend and soul-mate as well as her business partner. She returned to work at her charities and three months after Roger's passing, she became chairperson at 'Beyond Blue'.

These activities enabled Jan not to dwell on her loss during the day but at night she was quite often grief-stricken and lonely.

Blind Date

Chapter 26

Twelve months had passed when her best friend, Trish, suggested she start looking for a male companion.

'Jan, darling, you're a very attractive fifty-six year-old woman; you would have no trouble attracting a suitable man.'

'Don't be daft, Trish, I don't want to meet anybody. For God's sake, who could replace Roger?'

'I'm not suggesting you could ever replace Roger but you're spending a lot of time on your own. If you met a man, you could go out to restaurants, the theatre and generally he could keep you company.'

'No, I'm not interested.'

'OK, please yourself.'

Another twelve months passed and Jan's life remained much the same; she did miss not having an intelligent conversation with a man but then again she had lots of female friends she could talk to. She admitted to herself it wasn't the same as conversing with a male.

Trish and Jan were having lunch at Balmoral beach when Jan brought up the subject of dating.

'If I wanted to, where could I find a suitable man? I'm not going to front up to a nightclub in the hope someone will pick me up.'

'No, of course not, darling, you've got to get with the times. Internet dating is the way to go.'

'Oh no. I've read about all sorts of things going wrong through meeting a stranger on the net.'

'Some sites are better than others but the more reputable ones are very good.'

'Which ones?'

'I believe eHarmony and RSVP are the two most popular ones. I think the key is taking it slowly and not divulging too much about yourself. Certainly not your wealth.'

'Anything else?'

'Yes, if you progress to actually meeting someone, for the first time, do it at a restaurant and take me with you. There's safety in numbers.'

'I might give it a try.'

'Good girl. Keep me posted.'

Jan decided to sign up to eHarmony; the television ads looked convincing and she felt she had nothing to lose.

Their blurb said; 'to help you find a happy lasting relationship, we need to get to know you first. Our scientific Relationship Questionnaire allows us to do this at an unprecedented level of depth - it's one of the key reasons eHarmony's Compatibility Matching System™ has produced so many successful, lasting relationships.

After completing the questionnaire, you instantly receive your free, in-depth Personality Profile. This gives you deep insights into who you are and how others perceive you, as well as what your needs are in a partner.'

Jan completed the questionnaire and submitted her answers; within twenty-four hours, she received he profile back. It was quite uncanny how accurate it was.

The next day she received an email with four potential candidates. One stood out in particular: John Bennett. He was very good looking, aged fifty-eight and had his own recruitment company. He had travelled extensively and was looking for a partner who enjoyed travelling and going to the theatre. Jan thought he sounded very promising so she paid her subscription fees and agreed that John could contact her.

The first Internet chat was quite guarded; neither of them had used a service like eHarmony before. However, the chat was good enough for them to agree to chat again. Over the next month they chatted twice a week and discovered a lot more common interests. Jan discovered that John had a son who suffered from bi-polar disorder and been helped by the 'Beyond Blue' organisation. She also discovered he was a member of the same golf club where Roger had been a member. He didn't know Roger well but had played against him in competition; on both occasions, Roger had won.

Jan and John finally agreed to meet face- to- face after several telephone conversations.

Jan suggested the Boat Shed Restaurant in Neutral Bay. John agreed and the date was set: Saturday, 10th February.

Jan rang Trish to give her the news and invite her to join them.

Trish picked up her friend and drove to the restaurant. Both women were very nervous.

'You haven't even shown me his photo, Jan. Come on, let's see the hunk,' joked Trish after parking the Mercedes.

'Here it is. I don't know if he's been airbrushed; he might have a big wart on the end of his nose.'

'He's gorgeous. He looks a bit like George Clooney.'

'Yeah, he does a bit. Come on, let's see what he's really like.'

The two women entered the restaurant looking around the tables to see if they could spot him. A gentleman resembling George Clooney stood up and beckoned them over to the table. He held out their chairs while they were seated and asked if they would care for a wine. Both ladies requested a Riesling.

The conversation was relaxed and fluid, while John was extremely charming and obviously intelligent.

At the end of the lunch he shook both their hands and asked Jan if he could see her again; she agreed.

The next twelve months saw them progress from an eHarmony introduction to committed friends and lovers.

One Sunday evening at Jan's place, John got down on his knee and proposed. Jan was taken aback; this was a complete surprise to her.

'John, I don't know what to say.'

'You can say 'yes'.'

'I hope you will understand if I say I would like to think about it for a little while. I'd also like to talk to Kate.'

'I understand completely, my love. Take your time; I'm not going anywhere.'

Jan lay in her bed that night alone. She had asked John for some space. One side of her was happy and excited but the other felt she would be betraying Roger.

She telephoned Kate the next day and arranged to meet her in Kate's lunch break.

Jan explained the situation to her daughter and asked for her advice; she also asked her about her own feelings if she remarried.

'Mum, my initial reaction is, do it. You are a beautiful vibrant woman who deserves to be happy. Dad would be happy for you. He didn't expect you to become a Nun. I like John and he obviously loves you. You deserve to be loved, Mum.'

'I was hoping you would say that, darling, I was afraid you may not approve.'

'Well, I *do* approve. Now when's the wedding?'

'Oh my goodness, I haven't even accepted yet, let alone set a date.'

Jan did accept, much to John's delight. They began to plan the wedding, which they decided would be a small intimate affair. A restaurant they frequented was The Boat House on Neutral Bay. It was the place where they first met it seemed like a very appropriate venue.

The date was set for 28th February and the invitations went out to the thirty invitees. Trish was to be a witness and John selected his son, David.

The day before the ceremony, John called around to see Jan.

'Hello, darling, you still want to marry me?'

'Of course I do.'

'Well that's good, seeing I've just bought the tickets for our honeymoon.'

'What honeymoon? We never discussed a honeymoon.'

'You can't have a wedding without a honeymoon, darling.'

'So where are we going?'

'First we fly to London where we have five days then we catch the train to Paris and stay there for four days. I've hired a car so we can drive through France at our leisure and into Italy. We stay in Venice for three days then we drive to Florence for a day and finally Rome, where we stay for three days. We fly home via Hong Kong, where we stay for three days. We fly business class and the accommodation I've booked is first class.'

'John you've over whelmed me with your generosity. Thank you.'

'You're worth it, sweetheart.'

The wedding went as planned The guests were asked not to give presents but to make a donation to one of Jan's charities.

Overall, it was a wonderful day.

Happy Ever After
That's the Theory
Chapter 27

Jan and John left for their honeymoon five days after their wedding day; they stopped over in Dubai and stayed in the "Burj Al Arab" one of the most photographed buildings in the world.

John was in awe when he saw Tiger Woods and his entourage in the foyer of the hotel. He had just absorbed that fact when in walked Rory McElroy and Adam Scott. He approached the concierge and asked him why all the celebrity golfers? The concierge explained the Dubai Desert Classic was due to begin the following day.

John wished he had done his research a little more thoroughly so that they could have stayed for an extra day and watched the first day's play.

The newly-weds were picked up outside the hotel in a gold-coloured Hummer; they were going on a desert safari. The drive out to the desert took them a little under an hour then the fun began, climbing huge sand dunes and screaming down them and up again. After a couple of hours they stopped at a camp where cold drinks were offered as well as some Arabian snacks. Jan hoped they didn't include goats' eyes.

Their guide suggested the couple partake in a camel ride but both declined.

The two lovers returned to the hotel and slept for a couple of hours. Their flight to London was due to depart Dubai at ten pm.

When they arrived in London, a suite at Claridges awaited them.

Shopping in Oxford Street and Regent Street kept Jan happy, as did Savile Row for John.

They hired a car and drove to Oxford and spent a very pleasant day there, including a punt on the river Cherwell.

Jan had never been to Cornwall despite having ancestry from this beautiful area, so she requested they drive south and discover the coast. Her ancestors mainly came from a little village called St Ives, where they were due to stay at Trevose Harbour House, a five star retreat right on the water.

The origin of St Ives is attributed in legend to the arrival of the Irish Saint, in the 5th century. Walking around the village and the harbour filled Jan with a feeling of belonging. This was her family history.

The next stop was Padstow where they stopped for lunch at Rick Stein's Café for a delicious seafood meal. John ordered lightly curried crab mayonnaise with tomato. Jan chose crispy fried whole sea bass with a hot, sweet and sour sauce.

Boscastle was the village they chose to end their day and bed down for the night.

Jan liked the look of The Riverside Inn, a historic hotel with a four star rating; she chose well.

Next morning they drove back to London and checked into Claridges once more; they were due to catch the Chunnel train to Paris the next day.

They caught the train to Paris and despite both of them having visited the city of lights several times before, they enjoyed the museums and art galleries and, of course, the Parisian food.

The final night in Paris was spent dining in their hotel, the Champs Elysees Plaza; at six hundred dollars a night they thought a night in and ordering room service would make a nice change. The bill came to one hundred and eighty dollars, not much less than eating out. They both agreed Paris was beautiful but expensive.

John hired a BMW Five Series to drive through France and onto Geneva where they stopped for the night. They had booked a classic old hotel as their accommodation: Hotel d'Angleterre which lived up to its opulent reputation. Both Jan and John decided they would eat out of the hotel in a restaurant that reflected old Geneva. The concierge suggested L'Entrecote Couronnee. They were delighted with his recommendation as the décor was classic and the food was delicious.

The following morning they walked through the old city and visited the famous lake. The journey continued on to Venice, a six-hour drive; the travellers arrived at dusk. The BMW was handed back to the hire company at the airport where they caught a water Taxi to their hotel. John had chosen a luxury boutique hotel Ca' Pisani, a restored thirteenth century Venetian manor house. Jan was delighted. Neither Jan nor John had been to Venice before and therefor enjoyed taking a gondola ride around the ancient canals and visiting the Doge's Palace in St Mark's square. High on John's to do list was to visit Murano Island and discover how the Venetian glass was made into such exquisite forms. Jan purchased a set of twelve Venetian wine glasses to be shipped back home.

The next stop was Florence, where John hired another car, a red Alpha Romeo; he wanted to feel Italian for a few days.

The drive took them only three hours; more frustrating was the hour it took to find their accommodation, Hotel Principe, a small elegant hotel built in 1860 as a palatial home on the Arno River.

Their day in Florence was filled with the history of this beautiful city, the Ponte Vecchio, a visit to the famous Uffizi Gallery and finally, waiting in line for an hour to enter the Academia to view Michelangelo's David.

The end of their European tour was drawing to a close; they drove the Alpha the three hours to Rome. John may have been frustrated driving in Florence, but Rome was a different level altogether. Jan thanked God it wasn't her driving in the traffic, which could best be described as chaos.

John once again had found the most beautiful hotel, keeping his reputation well and truly intact; the Hotel Kolbe was a fifth-century convent-turned-hotel, regarded as Rome's best luxury small hotel.

In the three days in Rome they visited many of the sites including the Colosseum. Jan had heard about the town of Tivoli where the Roman elite, including Caesar, would stay in the summer months to get away from Rome's heat and humidity.

They drove up to the delightful mountain town on the second day and lunched at Osteria La Briciola, a very well known Tivoli restaurant.

Their final day in Rome was spent wandering through some of the city's galleries and museums, including Ara Pacis, Borghese Gallery and Capitoline Museums.

By the end of the day, they both felt exhausted, and even though the hotel had a world-class restaurant, they ordered two steak sandwiches and went to bed early.

The next day they were due to depart for Hong Kong, a place John knew very well as he had stayed there many times before on business.

A Rolls Royce from the Peninsula Hotel was waiting for them when they touched down and drove them to the world famous hotel. Once they were checked in and were shown their suite, John announced they would be dining at the world-renowned restaurant, "The Caprice", a three Michelin Star establishment that served both Chinese and French cuisine.

The two honeymooners enjoyed their stay in Hong Kong, riding the train up to the peak and shopping in the myriad of high-end shops. John had waited until they reached "Honkers" to purchase Jan's engagement ring; he knew a very famous jeweller from his days travelling to the island. They chose a large baguette diamond surrounded by smaller baguettes designed to simulate an art nouveau classic ring.

On their last night in the former colony John had arranged a special evening. He kept it as a surprise for Jan. After all, they were flying home to Sydney the next day, so this marked the end of their honeymoon.

He arranged for one of the Peninsula's Rolls Royces to pick them up and drive them to Pier Number 1, Tsim Sha Tsui. When they arrived they discovered moored the most beautiful Chinese junk, the "Aqua Luna".

The captain helped them aboard and explained they would be sailing out to the far end of the harbour and then would follow the coastline back to the pier.

Jan thought this was wonderful, sailing on the harbour with the island's lights reflecting on the water, a truly special moment to finish a wonderful trip.

The captain, Joseph Ho, brought out a bottle of Dom Pérignon and two crystal flute glasses. He had already poured the champagne in the galley so there was little chance of spillages. He handed a glass to Jan and one to John, wishing them well. Jan savoured the magnificent champagne: she was feeling on top of the world.

The captain appeared again and offered them another glass which Jan accepted, while John declined on the basis that he needed to visit the bathroom.

Jan sat at the back of the junk, the wind blowing her hair and her mood ecstatic, listening to the junk moving through the water. However, she began to feel dizzy and when she tried to stand, she fell onto the deck and lost consciousness.

John and Joseph quickly appeared and Joseph checked her pulse, which was very weak.

They pulled a body bag from under the seat and placed Jan's limp body into it. Joseph attached fifty kilos of lead weight to the bag and they then struggled to lift Jan over the side. Finally they succeeded and the two murderers watched as the bag, with a rope attached, began its descent.

They cleaned up the evidence, replacing the drugged champagne with a fresh bottle, with only a few drops left. The glasses were disposed of and replaced.

The junk motored on for a further five kilometres, heading towards a remote section of the shoreline. They anchored and hauled Jan back on board, removed her from the bag, then placed her in the junk's tender which was powered by a ten horsepower outboard motor. The two men headed for the shore where they beached the small boat and removed the dead woman, placing her strategically on the beach. Joseph knew these waters well; the tide and the currents would have more than likely washed her up on this shoreline. The police would not question her location. John and Joseph returned to the spot near where Jan had been murdered, reporting her missing to the police using Joseph's cell phone. The police launch arrived thirty minutes later with the officers taking down both their statements. It was obvious that Jan had drunk too much champagne and somehow lost her balance, probably hitting her head, and had fallen overboard. The police and the junk searched for several hours and gave up hope. The police decided they would try to find her body next day in the daylight.

John received a phone call about ten am the following day from the police, asking him to meet them at South Bay Beach as they suspected they had found Jan's body. He caught a taxi to the remote beach and was met by a senior police officer who led him down to where Jan had been located by a walker earlier that morning.

The police officer pulled back the blanket to reveal Jan's pure white and pallid face. John sunk to his knees and screamed. He was inconsolable, with tears streaming down his contorted face. He was led away from the scene by the police officer and placed in a police car for the trip back to the station, to give a statement.

Jan was transported to the morgue where a post mortem was conducted the following day. The Coroner's decision was "death by drowning".

John decided to have Jan cremated in Hong Kong and bring the ashes home, for obvious reasons, even though the ancient Chinese drug used to dope her was undetectable in the body after two hours of ingestion.

He booked his flight for the following Monday, enabling him time to get his affairs in order, including paying Joseph his US$50,000 fee for services rendered.

John was lamenting to himself about the amount of money he had expended on this project but the return on investment would be enormous. When he hatched his evil plan, he knew he would need to spend a considerable amount to prove his wealth to Jan. She wasn't interested in a gold digger. John didn't have the money required, so he borrowed $500,000 from a business associate who had links to organised crime, with a promise of a large return. He wasn't particularly worried as he knew he was due to inherit fifty per cent of Jan's cash fortune, based on their agreement before the marriage.

John settled into his business class seat. Of course Jan's seat had been sold, so he hoped he didn't get some fat boring bastard sitting next to him.

He was pleasantly surprised when a very attractive Chinese woman in her thirties sat down.

The two business class travellers didn't converse much at first but when the evening meal was served and both had a glass of very good wine, John started up a conversation.

'So are you travelling to Sydney on a holiday or business?'

'Business.'

'Just in Sydney or do you intend to visit other states?'

'I'm going to Melbourne and Brisbane also.'

'Do you mind if I ask you what you do?'

'Not at all. I'm a financial analyst with HSCB.'

'Big bank.'

'Yes.'

'You'll have to excuse me, I am a 'head hunter' My late wife used to chastise me for interviewing people.'

'That's OK, I don't mind. How long have you been a widower?'

'Oh, too long.'

'I see.'

'By the way, my name is John.'

'Hello, John, I'm Sue.'

The conversation went on for the majority of the flight. When they were due to land, John suggested he show Sue around Sydney. She accepted and plans were made for John to meet her in the foyer of the Regent Hotel on the following Saturday.

John passed through immigration and customs quickly and, there to greet him, were Kate and Steve. They all hugged, with tears streaming down their faces, consoling each other.

The three collected his luggage, including one of Jan's bags with her personal items that he felt Kate would like.

Sue looked on in bewilderment.

On the way home to John's apartment, he continued to sob.

> 'I just can't get used to the idea she's gone.'

> 'Neither can we, John, neither can we,' Kate sympathised.

> 'We were coming to the end of the most wonderful honeymoon, then she was gone. We were both looking forward to spending the rest of our lives together. How in the hell could this happen?'

Kate and Steve accompanied John into his apartment. Kate made them all a cup of tea and after an hour, they left him to his grief.

Unbeknown to Kate or Steve, Jan's close friend and business advisor, Graham Richards, had taken the liberty of hiring a private investigator to determine if John's account of what had happened to Jan was correct. The facts were that she met him through the Internet, her personal wealth was estimated at over fifty million dollars and she died mysteriously in Hong Kong on her honeymoon. Also, against his advice, she'd changed her will, leaving John fifty per cent of her liquid assets but at least her property assets were excluded. The firm he chose, "Bishop and Unger", were regarded as the best investigative agency in the world, with offices all over the globe, including Hong Kong. One of their most experienced Hong Kong agents was a very attractive, intelligent woman named Sue.

Kate and Steve arranged a memorial service in St Mary's Cathedral, the same church where her father's funeral was held. Over six hundred people attended and the wake was held at "Boat Shed Restaurant" the same venue where she was married, just two months prior. One hundred close friends and family attended.

After a few days, Kate and Steve and John attended a meeting at Jan's lawyers to hear the reading of the will. John, in particular, was keen to find out the exact amount he had inherited.

The lawyers, Smith and Schneiderman, were located on the thirtieth floor at three hundred Macquarie Street Sydney.

The three beneficiaries were surprised to see several other people in the reception area waiting to attend the same reading. Finally, they were all called into the large meeting room. All parties were seated at the long boardroom table, eagerly waiting to hear Jan's will.

Mr Schneiderman opened the proceedings with genuine condolences to John, Kate and Steve.

He addressed John first, confirming that fifty per cent of the money in Jan's estate would go to him. He then announced the remaining fifty per cent would go to her daughter, Kate.

No mention of the actual amount was declared.

The lawyer then decreed that the six charities she had supported would all receive a donation of five million dollars, these charities being:

Beyond Blue
Salvation Army
Sydney Children's Hospital
The Smith Family
The Cancer Council
The Fred Hollows Foundation

He then announced that Jan had recently purchased three large nursing homes with significant dementia wings. These facilities were located in: The Blue Mountains, "Blue Haven Nursing Home; Melbourne, "Green Ferns"and Brisbane, "Brookfield".

In addition, three significant medical centres were purchased in Sydney at Bondi Junction, North Sydney and Parramatta.

These medical facilities were left to her daughter Kate and her husband, Steve, on condition that they managed them on a full time basis.

'So, that brings me to declare the cash component of the will, after donations as outlined, the amount left in Jan's bank account was $50,000. Under the terms of the will, as outlined previously, Mr Bennett receives $25,000, as does Mrs Wilson's daughter.

That, ladies and gentlemen, brings us to the conclusion of the meeting. Good afternoon.'

162

'Excuse me, Mr Schneiderman, may I speak with you in private?'

'Yes, Mr Bennett, come into my office.'

Sir, I am very disturbed by the nature of my wife's will.'

'How so?'

'I was under the distinct impression Jan had several millions in her bank account but now I find she has frittered it all away. How am I going to live?'

'By all accounts, Mr Bennett, you are a wealthy man in your own right. That's why Mrs Wilson decided to give the majority of her fortune to charities and to her daughter.'

'Well, I can assure you, I will be contesting this wretched will.'

'Contesting wills that have been clear in their intention can be a risky and expensive business. However, it's your money, Mr Bennett.'

He Who Lives by the Sword Dies by the Sword

Chapter 28

John returned home to his apartment, grabbed a bottle of Scotch and poured himself a large glass. He sat on the lounge and contemplated his future; he was broke, apart from his 'fucking piddling inheritance' from his once dear wife. He had committed murder on the basis he would receive significant financial benefit. He owed $500,000 to the mob, with no chance of repaying it.

All in all, his future looked pretty damn good. He poured himself another Scotch and tried to come up with a solution. There was none; he was well and truly ruined. His biggest fear was being tortured by the thugs who lent him the money and he was terrified of dying a slow horrible death; these bastards don't muck around.

He had a third drink, wrote a note, then grabbed his car keys. He drove to the eastern suburbs where a famous suicide spot called "The Gap" was located. He sat in the car for over an hour trying to come up with an alternative: there was none.

He opened the car door, climbed over the fence, looked down into the dark abyss and jumped. Joggers running along the cliff-top pathway next morning spotted the body on the rocks below and called the police.

The Rose Bay police arrived within the hour and Special Forces abseiled down the cliff and brought the body up in a stretcher.

John had left his wallet in his back pocket so identification and his address were easily determined.

The police went to his apartment, letting themselves in using the key on his key ring left in the ignition of his Audi.

On the coffee table was a note.

This is the last thing I will ever write.

I did murder my wife, Jan, hoping to inherit a fortune. The bitch was too smart for me.

The police can contact Joseph Ho in Hong Kong He's the skipper of the "Aqua Luna". He was my co-conspirator.

I have no alternative but to top myself. Good Bye cruel world

John Bennet

Based on the note and the evidence collected by Bishop and Unger there was no doubt Jan Wilson had been murdered by her husband, John Bennett, and Joseph Ho for monetary gain.

The case was closed and Kate and Steve tried to get on with their lives, including running their vast medical business.

Business is Business

Chapter 29

Kate and Steve were coming to grips with the vast medical group that had been left to them by Kate's mother, Jan. Neither of them had had any business experience: they were clinicians. After taking control, they decided to employ a recruitment company, Future Directions, to help them find a General Manager and several practice managers, one for each facility. After three months of searching and interviewing prospective candidates, they chose a management group they felt confident with. Kate and Steve would be joint Managing Directors.

The first thing on their agenda, once the management group was in place, was to hire a consulting company to conduct an audit on the practices used in each of the nursing homes and medical clinics. The audit took a month and the consultancy presented their findings at the July board meeting.

Overall, the report was favourable with the medical clinics receiving the greatest praise for their work practices.

The three nursing homes varied in their ratings, with Blue Haven being rated first and Brookfield last. However, all passed the audit. The most critical issue was over dispensing antipsychotic drugs to dementia patients. The report recommended that a review in each home take place to minimise their use.

Kate and Steve were concerned about unnecessary drug use and vowed to reduce the amount dispensed in each home. Overall they were pleased with the results contained in the report.

Life had certainly changed for the couple; they moved out of their rented apartment at McMahons point and purchased a stunning home at Whale Beach on the northern shore. The house was very modern with picture windows across the entire front of the building. The sea views were amazing; quite often they would be sitting at the breakfast bar when one of them would spot a pod of humpback whales swimming past. The surf beach at the bottom of their garden steps was a bonus for Steve who still surfed at every opportunity.

Tick Tock
Time Waits for No Man
Chapter 30

Rob and Henry were working ridiculous hours trying to redevelop AL252. They had tried several formulae but just when they thought they had a breakthrough, the mice would begin to regress. Rob had begun to notice the tell tale symptoms of Alzheimer's creeping back into his brain. It wasn't chronic but enough to alert him of what was to come if he and Henry didn't discover the rogue element that was negating the healing properties of the drug.

AL252 was thought to make it possible to target the toxic plaques that clump together in the brain and cause confusion and memory loss.

The research team believed it had worked out how a specific enzyme triggered the destruction of neurons in the brain. Rob, Henry and the team had obtained extraordinary knowledge about how the enzyme gamma secretase could be modulated. This was the knowledge they thought would be invaluable for them to further develop AS252.

Rob and Henry were under no illusion that scientists had been trying to target gamma secretase to treat Alzheimer's for over a decade. They thought they had cracked it.

It was their hypothesis that the next-generation molecules, by modulating rather than inhibiting the enzyme, could have few, if any, side effects.

Even though they were making good progress with their research they knew the clock was ticking down for Rob. If they didn't come up with the right formula, Rob would gradually deteriorate into an Alzheimer's induced haze for the rest of his short life.

The board had been following Rob's progress closely; he was required to give them monthly updates. As the months went by, the board could see the progress the disease was having on Rob just by his presentations; he began to become confused and forgot the simplest of words and phrases. The members of the board felt empathy for Rob but were also extremely concerned as their company had made an extensive investment in a drug they hoped would bring lucrative returns.

'Rob, I'm happy for you to try the latest version of AS252. The mice seem to be cured and, importantly, they haven't relapsed.'

'Henry why haven't you informed me of this before? Technically it's my fucking project.'

'Mate, I didn't want to get your hopes up and then find out it fails down the track just like before,'

'So you've been working on a derivative of the drug while I've been working on an entirely different formula?'

'One of us was going to crack it and in this instance, it was me. You know what? They say two heads are better than one.'

'I suppose you're right. I'm a bit testy at the moment as you no doubt know.'

'Ok, so are you happy to have another crack at it?'

'Does a bear shit in the woods? Of course I am. If you think you've finally cracked it, I'm your man.'

'Good. Well, mate, it's going to be the same process, a weekly injection with constant monitoring of progress.'

'Henry, just one thing. The only other person who has been on the AS252 program is, as you know, my mother. She has made unbelievable progress and both hers and my father's lives have turned around. I want her to start the program.'

'Yeah, I don't see a problem with that, mate.'

The following Monday Rob was injected with AS252-A. He continued on with his research in the hope that if this new derivative failed, his version might work.

There was no reduction in his work rate, a situation Andy was concerned about. Rob would get home late and leave for the Lab early, so that all in all, Rob was working sixteen hour days. Andy knew his partner couldn't continue at this pace. He had been on the new drug for two months and his progress was amazing. He was delighted.

One morning about seven a.m. Rob was driving to the Lab, taking his usual route through the back streets of McMahons Point heading for the Sydney Harbour Bridge.

Suddenly his whole body started shaking; he had lost complete control. The Alpha Spider smashed into a parked car and veered into another on the opposite side. Rob rolled over twice, resting on the Spider's roof; luckily, he didn't have the roof down.

A resident heard the accident and raced out to investigate. Fuel was spilling out of the petrol tank; his quick thinking saved Rob from the inferno which soon engulfed the motor vehicle. He undid the seatbelt and dragged Rob to safety. Another resident had called 000 and an ambulance soon arrived, as did the police. Rob was examined inside the ambulance and a quick diagnosis was made: his left arm had been broken and he had a suspected ruptured spleen. He was taken to the Royal North Shore hospital and taken to the emergency ward where several doctors examined him. It was agreed that Rob needed emergency surgery on his spleen or he could quite possibly die.

The surgery was successful and they didn't need to remove the spleen; instead, they arrested the bleeding by stitching the tear.

Rob spent the next week in hospital convalescing; his mother and father came to visit each day, as did Steve and Kate. He was astounded at how articulate his mother was; she seemed to be completely cured. It gave him great hope for his own recovery. He was eventually allowed to leave with strict instructions that he was to rest at home for a further three weeks.

Andy wheeled him out to the car which he had hired until they both decided what the next car would be. Andy found it difficult to get the patient into the front seat with an arm in plaster and an abdomen that was still very sore but finally he managed.

The two men arrived home and, with some difficulty, reached their apartment, Andy helped his lover onto the couch and suggested a coffee, which Rob enthusiastically agreed to.

'So, mate, do the doctors know what caused you to lose control at the wheel?'

'They ran some tests while I was in hospital and apparently I had a tonic-clonic seizure.'

'What the fuck is that?'

'It's an epileptic fit.'

'Shit, have you ever had one before? You know, as a kid or anything?'

'No.'

'Well do they say whether you're likely to have another one any time soon?'

'They don't know.

Can we talk about something else, Andy? I'm a bit over the whole fucking thing.'

'Sorry, mate, I'm just worried about you.'

'I know you are, Andy, but I'm sure everything will be fine.'

After Rob had been at home for a few days, he received a visit from Henry.

'Well, mate, how are you feeling? You look OK apart from the plaster on your arm.'

'Yeah I'm OK, mate, just still a bit sore around the tummy.'

'Well, that's to be expected. You ruptured your bloody spleen.'

'I guess so.'

'The doctors have informed me you had a tonic-clonic seizure. That's a big one, Rob. You could have easily been killed if it had happened on the bridge.'

'Well, it didn't happen while I was driving on the bridge.'

'Do you have any idea what brought it on? You have no previous history of epilepsy.'

'No idea.'

'Mate, I think we both know what instigated the attack: AS252-A. The brain has somehow got out of kilter and the electrics are beginning to get confused.'

'What are you trying to tell me, Henry?'

'I have to take you off the program. It's just too dangerous.'

'If you do that, you're sentencing me to a life of dementia. I'll be in a fucking nursing home where you might come and visit me on occasion, sitting with the other Alzheimer's patients, dribbling on my pyjamas and watching old re-runs of Dad's fucking Army. No way'

'I'm sorry, Rob. That's the way it's got to be.'

Henry said good-bye and went down to his car, got in and sobbed for a full thirty minutes. Rob did the same.

Rob was dreading telling Andy; he knew what effect it would have on his partner and their long-term future.

Andy returned home from work to find Rob on the couch drinking a Scotch and looking mournful.

'Well, it's nice for some. I've been flat out at work and here you are having a drink before I get home. What's going on?'

Rob looked up at his mate and Andy could see he had been crying.

'What's up, mate? I was only joking. You can have a drink whenever you like.'

'It's not you, Andy, it's me. Henry came to visit me today and informed me he was taking me off the program.'

'Why?'

'He's worried that I will have more fits while I'm on the drug. He thinks it could be fatal.'

172

'Well maybe it's better than what you can look forward to for the rest of your life.'

'It's not just me, to be fair. He has to consider the overall research program and the thousands of sufferers who will be affected if the program is closed down.'

'So what happens now?'

'What happens now is I will gradually get worse and eventually go into Blue Haven where I'll slowly decline and die. Andy, you are reasonably young and fit so I don't expect you to stay with me and watch me deteriorate.'

'Don't be so fucking ridiculous, Rob, I'm here for the long haul. You're my soul mate, my partner for life. I don't want to hear any more of this bullshit.'

Andy knew that he had to continue to work to keep the household going. When it came the time that Rob couldn't cope, he would have to go into the nursing home. He hoped that would be a few years away.

Rob resigned from his position at DRC, something he hoped he wouldn't have to do. He was now a stay- at- home partner of Andy's, except he couldn't cook anymore, at least not after he left the roast chicken on high for four hours and nearly burnt the place down. He progressively got worse and his latest assessment rated him at stage four, approaching stage five.

Andy came home one evening when the outside temperature was fifteen degrees Celsius. It was mid-winter and rain was falling heavily. He entered the apartment expecting a beautiful ambient heat of about twenty degrees; instead, it felt like a fridge. Rob was sitting in the lounge room in a t-shirt and board shorts with thongs on his feet. Andy had to explain that it was winter and they needed to turn up the heat. Andy was concerned that these occurrences were becoming more frequent. He decided to contact Steve and get his advice.

'Hello, Steve. It's Andy. I was wondering if I could meet you for a coffee tomorrow. I need to talk to you about Rob.'

'Is everything all right, mate?'

'No, not really, that's why we need to talk.'

'OK, Andy, why don't you meet me at "Aromas" in Chatswood, say about ten?'

'That sounds good, Steve. See you then.'

Steve arrived at the coffee shop just after ten and found Andy sitting in a booth down the back.

'G'day, Andy, have you ordered yet?'

'No, mate, I was waiting for you.'

'What would you like?'

'Just a double shot flat white thanks, Steve.'

Steve went up to the counter and ordered the coffees; he also ordered two Florentines.

'So, what's up with my big brother?' asked Steve as he sat down in the booth.

'To be frank, Steve, it's all getting too hard. I have to work five and a half days a week and lately I'm worried about leaving him alone. I can't bear the thought of putting him into a nursing home but it seems like there is no other alternative.'

'I was afraid he might be getting too difficult for you to handle. There is an alternative to a nursing home, albeit one of ours.'

'Pray tell?'

'Kate and I have discussed this; we think if we seconded one of our best nurses to be with Rob during the day, it would alleviate the fear you have of him being alone. If you wish, we could try and find one of our staff to be a live-in. That would give you total support.'

'Mate, that would be wonderful. Can I think about whether we should have day or live-in support?'

'Sure, let me know when you've made your decision.'

The two men left Aromas and went their separate ways. Andy got home at the usual time only to find soapsuds all over the kitchen floor and seeping into the lounge room carpet. He asked Rob what had happened?

'I'm sorry, Andy. I thought I'd surprise you by doing the washing before you got home.'

Rob had squeezed most of the dirty clothes from the basket into the dishwasher and poured half a bottle of detergent into it before pushing the Wash button. He didn't use dishwasher detergent; if he had, it wouldn't be quite the disaster it had turned out to be.

Andy cleaned up the mess, being careful not to show his annoyance to Rob. What this episode did do was to cement his opinion that a live-in nurse was the answer.

He rang Andy the next morning, recounting the latest episode and requesting a live-in nurse.

'The only real concern I have, Steve, is the cost.'

'No need to worry about the cost, Andy. Kate and I are more than happy to cover it.'

'That's great, mate. I really do appreciate it.'

'Not at all, mate. After all, he's my brother.'

Steve and Kate discussed who the likely candidate could be; obviously it had to be an experienced dementia nurse. The other prerequisite was that the person had to be single.

Take Good Care

Chapter 31

The two of them interviewed four candidates and agreed to offer the position to Geoff Abraham from their Blue Haven facility.

An interview with Andy and Geoff was organised at the apartment. Rob and Andy had sold the Crow's Nest apartment the previous year and purchased a three-bed unit at North Bridge with wonderful views over Sailors Bay.

Geoff caught a taxi to the apartment, impressed with the area and the views.

He rang the doorbell and Andy opened the door.

'Hello, I'm Andy. You must be Geoff, come on in.'

'Thanks, Andy.'

'Can I offer you a coffee?'

'Yes thanks. I'd love one.'

'How do you take it?'

'White, no sugar thanks.'

While Andy was making the coffee, Geoff walked out to the balcony, admiring the view over the bay.
Rob hadn't surfaced from the bedroom as he hated having visitors.

'Take a seat, Geoff; Steve and Kate have recommended you highly. I believe you have fifteen years' nursing experience, ten of which have been caring for dementia patients.'

'That's correct, Andy, it was what I wanted to do right from the beginning of my career.'

'Why dementia?'

'My Grandfather and Grandmother both died from Alzheimer's and it had a lasting effect on me. I wanted to make a difference.'

'Good reason. How do you feel about living here in somebody else's environment?'

'Well, if you're living away from home, this is a pretty good environment to live in.'

'OK, let me show you around. The apartment was used by the previous owners to provide a home for the wife's mother. Therefore there is a granny flat configuration; as you can see, you have your own kitchenette and good sized bathroom coming off a Queen sized bedroom. You have your own Juliette balcony with bay glimpses. My God, I sound like a real estate agent.'

'Not at all, this would be fine, very comfortable. Is the television connected to Foxtel?'

'No, but we can arrange it if you wish.'

"It's about all I watch these days. Free-to-air has become so naff.'

'I agree, we watch Foxtel probably ninety per cent of the time.'

'Speaking of 'we', can I meet Rob?'

'Yes, of course. Let's go into the lounge room and I'll see if I can coax him out. He's a little wary of strangers.'

Andy went into the bedroom and asked Rob to join him and a friend.

'What fucking friend? We don't have any friends.'

'Don't be silly, we have lots of friends. His name is Geoff and he'd really like to meet you, mate. Come on.'

Rob reluctantly walked out of the bedroom into the lounge room and sat heavily on the chair opposite Geoff and Andy on the sofa.

'So, Rob, Geoff would like to ask you a few questions.'

'Why, so he can put me in a fucking nursing home? That's it, isn't it? This prick is going to take me away. Well I can tell you now, I'm not fucking going anywhere.'

'Rob, calm down, mate. You're not going anywhere. Geoff is here to see if he'd like to stay here a while as our flat mate,'

'That's right, mate, and guess what, I've decided to stay. Is that OK with you?'

'I suppose so.'

'Right. Well that's settled,' said Andy with some relief.

As Geoff was leaving, Andy felt it was necessary to reassure him.

'He's not usually like that, mate, he's just paranoid about going into a nursing home and losing his freedom.'

'I can understand that it's going to take a little time but I'm sure it will all be fine. When do you want me to move in?'

'Would the weekend suit you?'

'Perfect, say Saturday afternoon?'

'Done.'

Geoff moved into the granny flat; by the end of the day, he had unpacked his things and settled in. The agreement he had struck with Andy meant the weekends were his own; he was required to work Monday to Friday.

Geoff left the apartment, informing Andy and Rob he would be back early Monday morning.

He had his own apartment in Springwood in the Blue Mountains; he was keen to spend the weekends there.

On Monday morning at 8am Geoff arrived at Andy and Rob's apartment ready to start his new role as nurse to Rob.

Both Rob and Andy were sitting at the breakfast bar finishing their breakfast. Andy asked Geoff if he would like a coffee which he accepted as he sat down next to Rob.

'So, mate, how are you today?'

'I'm OK, I suppose. Do you know I've got Alzheimer's?'

'Yes. Andy did mention it to me. Are you coping with it all right?'

'Not really.'

'How come?'

'How come? You try it, arsehole, and see how you like it.'

'Sorry, Rob, I didn't mean it.'

Andy broke up the conversation by bringing the coffee over for them both.

'Right, you guys, behave yourselves while I'm at work, OK?'

'Don't worry, we will,' said Rob.

'Do you want me to do anything for you during the day? I'm quite happy to do the shopping; it's a good outing for Rob.'

'Oh I hadn't thought of that. Well yes, I've made up the shopping list but I don't have any cash on me. I usually put it on my debit card.'

'That's OK, mate. I'll keep the receipt and you can reimburse me.'

'Great, that saves me doing it in my lunch hour.'

Andy left for work feeling comfortable that Geoff would be able to cope with Rob despite the occasional outburst.

He rang Geoff at lunchtime to see how things were going. He was pleased to hear that Geoff had brought out a big box of Lego and Rob was enjoying making various things, none of which was recognizable.

At two pm Geoff got Rob organised to go and do the grocery shopping at the local supermarket. Rob enjoyed any outing in the car so he was quite the willing shopper.

Once they got the shopping trolley, the adventure began.

This was to be the first time Rob had entered a supermarket since he had been diagnosed; as soon as Geoff and he entered this frightening place, things got difficult.

Rob didn't like the piped music and made it known to everybody in the store.

> 'Shut that fucking horrible music up!' he yelled at the top of his voice.

Geoff was sure that most shoppers in the place agreed with him but...

Geoff tried to calm him down but the obstacles in the middle of the aisles were making him even more agitated. They managed to reach the fruit and vegetables but Rob kept picking up products that weren't on the list; Geoff returned the turnips amongst other things, however Rob became abusive, accusing Geoff of trying to make him look stupid. Finally Geoff gave up; he left the trolley in the aisle and made a speedy exit, never to return with Rob in tow.

The best solution, Geoff thought, was to take him for a drive; Geoff made his way to Manly Beach where they stopped and bought a gelato ice cream. The two men walked along the esplanade, sitting down on a park bench to watch the surfers.

After about an hour, they drove back to North Bridge; Rob was perfectly happy.

Andy arrived home at the usual time, not knowing what to expect. He was pleasantly surprised to see both of them on the sofa watching The World From Above on Foxtel. Rob seemed to be entranced with the aerial views of England with the old castles and enormous manor homes. Andy smelled wonderful aromas coming from the kitchen; he said his 'hellos' and went in to investigate. Geoff had a large pot of spaghetti simmering on the stove.

> 'Geoff, I don't expect you to cook. You're Rob's carer not our house-keeper.'

> 'I know, mate, but I like cooking and Rob enjoys helping me, so why not?'

> 'Well I really appreciate it but don't make it a habit, will you?'

'We'll see.'

'How did you go with the shopping?'

'Not good.'

Geoff recounted the shopping disaster, blow by blow.

'OK, I'll do the shopping from now on. It's no big deal. I'll just stop on the way home as I've been doing all along.'

'Sure and I'll do the majority of the cooking. Do you like filet au poivre?'

'I love it and I know Rob also enjoys it. I've cooked it for him plenty of times.'

'Great, I'll pick up some eye fillet from the butcher's tomorrow.'

Geoff served up the meal and the three men sat down to a delicious French meal complemented by a fine red wine.

The new regime was working well with the demarcation of roles accepted by Andy and Geoff.

Rob tended to go off to bed straight after dinner; he'd watch television for an hour and drift off to sleep. Andy and Geoff would talk for hours and discover they had a lot in common, including being gay.

As the months rolled by, Rob became more difficult for both Geoff and Andy to handle.

'Andy, I think we need to consider Rob going into Blue Haven; in my opinion, he is already at stage five. That's more than I can handle on my own during the day.'

'Bugger, I was dreading this day. I know he has a deep fear of living in a nursing home.'

'I don't think anybody looks forward to it but you have to be practical.'

'I suppose you're right; damn it.'

'If it's any consolation, you have the knowledge that I'll be working there. I'll make sure he's looked after. Not only that... his brother owns the fucking joint!'

Andy laughed but deep down he was dreading telling his partner he was moving into a nursing home.

That night after Rob retired, the two men sat drinking whisky and discussing the logistics of the move. After one glass too many, Geoff made a startling announcement.

'Andy, I find you very attractive. Would you ever consider entering into a relationship with me?'

'Geoff, I don't think it appropriate that we should even be discussing it while my long-term partner is still alive.'

'I'm sorry, Andy, you're right. I'm totally out of line.'

'Geoff, I'm flattered that you find me attractive. If circumstances were different, I'd be keen I assure you.'

'Well, that makes me feel a little better. Thanks, Andy.'

The Fire of Jealousy

Chapter 32

Andy waited a few days just to convince himself he was doing the right thing; he concluded he was.

He telephoned Steve and discussed the situation with him so they agreed to meet the next day at Aromas.

Andy walked in and found Steve at their usual booth. He ordered two coffees and sat down opposite his lover's brother.

'Hi, Steve, how are you mate?'

'I'm good. What about you, more importantly?'

'Yeah, I'm just about coping.' A tear began running down his cheek.

'I know it must be very hard for you, Andy, but you've got a good support group.'

'Yeah I know, Steve. Thanks, mate.'

'When do you want to bring him into Blue Haven?'

'According to Geoff, the sooner the better.'

'Well, I can assure you that we'll treat him like a prince. We've got the best room in the house waiting for him.'

'I can't thank you and Kate enough for providing us with Geoff; he's been fantastic. Rob really likes him.'

'That's great, mate. It's our intention for Geoff to continue that role at Blue Haven.'

'Fantastic, that'll make it an easier transition.'

'I'll talk to Geoff and arrange for Rob to be transferred to the Blue Mountains in the next few days.'

'I really do appreciate your support, Steve.'

'Hey, he's my brother. He means the world to me as well.'

The day arrived when Rob was to be moved; he didn't need much persuasion. It was just another car trip to him.

Both Andy and Geoff were with him and kept him amused throughout the three-hour drive. It was only when they pulled into the portico of Blue Haven did he sense something was going on.

'Why are we stopping here?'

'We're going to visit an old friend,' said Andy.

'Who?'

'Brian. You remember Brian don't you?'

Brian had been a friend of their father and he was now a resident suffering from dementia.

'I don't remember him. Mind you, I don't remember any fucking thing.'

'Come on, let's go and see Brian. I'm sure you'll recognise him when you see him.'

'OK, but I don't want to stay for long. These places give me the creeps.'

The two men helped Rob out of the back seat of the car and assisted him up the ramp into reception. Steve was waiting for them.

'I know you! We go back a long way. What's your name?'

'My name is Steve. I'm your brother.'

'Are you?'

'I am. Why don't you come with me? I've got a special place to show you.'

The four of them walked down the corridor and into the dementia wing. Steve opened the door to what would be Rob's new home. It was a larger room than standard and had a large picture window overlooking the golf course. Andy had arranged to have photos and other personal items arranged around the room. There was a large television mounted to the wall opposite to where the bed was located. A two-seater and coffee table were arranged in the corner of the room.

'So, Rob, what do you think of your new home?' asked Andy.

'It's very nice.'

'Why don't you lie on the bed and have a little nap, mate. It's been a long trip.   You must be tired.'

Rob agreed and lay on the bed. Geoff took his shoes off. They all gradually moved out into the corridor and walked back to the reception area where Andy filled out and signed the necessary papers.

'It's going to take a little time but he'll fit into the routine,' said Geoff.

'Yeah I think you're right, Geoff. It's good you're here to give him the reassurance he needs,' said Steve.

A new chapter in Rob's life had begun. Dux of the school, University Medal, Doctorate in Medical Research, discoverer of a cure for Alzheimer's and now dementia patient and a resident at Blue Haven. Life's circle.

Rob fitted into the routine very well. He made new friends and enjoyed sitting in the television lounge and watching videos with the other residents.

His best friend was a bloke called Harry. Rob and he used to change the channels on the TV just to annoy the other residents.

Another trick they both played was to hide the spoons in their pockets and bury them in the garden. They were amused when the kitchen staff would complain that there were no spoons to eat dessert.

Harry and Rob's favourite DVD was André Rieu. The boys would sit in the lounge transfixed by André and all the pretty girls in their colourful frocks playing violin. The hid the remote when they were watching him. Their second favourite was Dad's Army; both men would laugh and laugh at their antics.

There were a couple of inmates they didn't much care for; one was Ron. He'd just yell and scream the whole time. Rob and Harry would tell him to shut up but it had no effect. The other one they didn't like was Sally. She'd just walk around all day with a blank look on her face and come up really close and fart: how disgusting they found it.

Geoff worked the day shift so he could keep an eye on Rob.

After about three months at Blue Haven, Rob started to feel restless in himself; he decided to break out and go back home to Andy and the apartment, which he still remembered.

He began watching the nursing staff key in the lock combination, memorising it long enough to be able to return to his room and write it down on a note pad.

He began to plan his escape and he chose Saturday morning as the day, although he didn't really know when that was.

Rob seemed settled when the nurse came in to make sure all was as it should be. She pulled the blankets up to his chin and wished him good night.

Rob could still read his digital watch so he kept looking at it until it reached two am. He sprang out of bed fully clothed and grabbed his plastic bag which had his essentials, including a toothbrush toothpaste and a toilet roll.

He opened his door slightly and peered both ways. The coast was clear so he headed for the door, took the note pad from his pocket and tapped in the numbers. Pushing the door quietly, he popped his head out. There was no one there. He quickly made his way through the foyer and down the front stairs, heading for the golf course. He had forgot to pack a torch, not that he owned one anyway; it was serendipity that it was a full moon. He started trotting along the first fairway, nearly falling into a bunker. Rob had no idea where he was heading: he only knew he needed to get as far away from Blue Haven as possible before dawn.

He had crossed over four fairways when he discovered a pathway leading into the bush. He staggered along the bush track, tripping over tree roots and rocks but he was able to stay upright until he tripped on a log that had fallen over the track during a recent storm. He went crashing down the embankment, landing awkwardly and breaking his leg. Rob lay there sobbing for the remainder of the night.

Geoff looked in on Rob first thing after he started his shift each morning. This particular morning, he found Rob missing from his room so he began a search of the dementia wing but couldn't find him anywhere. He raised the alarm and three other nurses joined the search; after about half an hour, they all concluded that Rob had escaped.

Initially they were not going to call the police but with the steep cliffs and bush land surrounding the nursing home, they decided to make the call.

The police arrived soon after and two officers, a male and a female officer, led the search. They first walked the road leading into the town of Leura and searched around the town itself: no Rob.

It was decided to call in the State Emergency Service (SES) to help search the bushland and the golf course. The SES sent six crew members to conduct the search and by lunchtime they discovered Rob down the bottom of the ditch. They checked his status and carried him out on a stretcher. An ambulance had been called when Rob had been located and was able to reach the track via the golf course. He was taken to Katoomba hospital a few kilometres away.

Rob remained in hospital for two days and then returned to Blue Haven with plaster on his leg.

Andy was extremely upset when he heard what had happened and made the decision to lease out the North Bridge apartment and rent a cottage in Leura so he could be closer to his soul-mate. He was able to secure a chemist's position at Katoomba while taking leave of absence from his management position at Chatswood.

Once Andy had moved closer to Rob, things settled down. He would visit the home every day and stay with Rob for a few hours each day.

His friendship with Geoff grew; they would eat together twice a week alternating between houses or frequenting the many fine restaurants in the area. Geoff was becoming more and more infatuated with Andy but Andy had made it clear from the outset that he had no intention of entering into another relationship while Rob was alive.

Geoff's infatuation grew into obsession and his attitude to Rob was affected by jealousy.

One night while Geoff was sitting in front of the cottage's open fire with his fourth Scotch in hand, he developed a plan that would solve his problem.

Obsession

Chapter 33

It was a particularly cold night in the Blue Mountains. Snow had been predicted although it hadn't fallen yet. Geoff packed his car with the necessary items which would allow him to carry out his plan; he drove to Blue Haven, arriving at three am. He parked his car a kilometre from the home and slunk up the street until he reached the entrance. Making sure no staff were in the reception area, he entered the building and opened the secure door to the dementia wing. Geoff made his way to Rob's room and entered; it was pitch black but he could hear Rob's breathing and knew he was asleep. Quietly he opened the door to the ensuite and found the wastebasket. The bag he carried had firelighters and combustible materials, which he shoved into the basket. This was the moment he had to decide whether he would go ahead with his shocking plan or would he retract and leave well alone? He decided to go ahead: this was the only way he and Andy could be together as partners. He lit the basket with a lighter, waited until the fire lighters were well alight and left the room with the ensuite door open. Quickly departing the nursing home, he ran to the golf course and stood on the first fairway so he could watch the building burn. His justification was that Rob was close to dying anyway, as were all the other residents. He was just helping things along a bit.

As Geoff stood there, he could see smoke emanating from the building. Smoke became flames and within a relatively short period of time, the building was entirely engulfed. In the distance he heard the sound of fire trucks but by the time they arrived it was too late. In the street outside the home, he could see a few nursing staff. Geoff hoped they were all out, as it was not his intention to kill them.

Eventually he made his way back to his car and drove home, pouring himself a large whisky with which he toasted a new beginning with Andy.

The fire-fighters were able to save fifteen of the thirty residents: no staff were killed.

The news reports were broadcast all over Australia and of course people were horrified such a thing could happen.

The Arson Squad examined the burnt-out building and concluded the fire had started in Rob's ensuite and had been deliberately lit. It was no longer a fire investigation: it was a murder investigation.

The police cordoned off the entire area and began interviewing staff, including Geoff. They had no real clues in the early stages of the investigation.

Andy had received a call from one of the nurses he knew well, soon after she was evacuated. He dressed and raced down to the scene only to find the building completely destroyed. He tried to enter but a police officer held him back.

'Officer, my friend is in there. I've got to try and get him out.'

'I'm sorry, sir. Nobody is allowed past the tape, it's just too dangerous.'

'I don't believe this. It's just too horrible.'

A police officer drove Andy home to his cottage and interviewed him. Once the interview was completed, Andy was left to grieve alone.

Rob's funeral was held the Friday after the fire, yet again, at St Mary's Cathedral. It was attended by four hundred people and, apart from family and friends, the DRC board, the Governor of New South Wales and several Federal MPs attended. Rob had been a much respected and loved human being.

Rob's parents, John and Bev, held the wake at their apartment for a few family and friends, including Geoff and Henry. It was Rob and Henry's research that had enabled Bev not only to be attending the wake but organising it.

The task force formed to find the murderer of fifteen people had grown to twenty; this was a crime that had to be solved.

They received plenty of leads but the one that drew their attention was that of a night-shift worker who had been returning home after his shift.

He saw a man park his car, a blue Corolla, in a side street about a kilometre from the nursing home. He watched as the man carrying a canvas bag walked towards Blue Haven. This witness lived two doors down from the aged care facility and was standing in his front yard having a cigarette when he saw the same man leave the home and walk over to the golf course. Even though it was dark, the streetlights illuminated his face: the man was the same one he saw being interviewed on television.

That man was Geoff.

The police went around to his cottage, knocked on the front door and asked to speak to him at the police station.

Geoff was confident he could not, and would not, be connected to the fire so he went with a sense of bravado.

After ten hours of questioning, Geoff confessed to the crime and was arrested. He was not granted bail.

He was tried six months later and received fifteen life sentences.

Although Andy, Steve and Kate were happy with the sentence, nothing could bring back Rob.

Steve and Kate felt a sense of responsibility and guilt for what had happened to Rob but a detailed inquiry exonerated them of any blame. Blue Haven was a well-run, adequately staffed facility with all the appropriate fire and smoke alarms. There was nothing their company could have done to improve the safety of their residents.

Dementia a Major Challenge

Chapter 34

Dementia threatens to be the major health care challenge for the world with no cause, cure or effective treatment.

Currently, about three hundred and thirty thousand Australians have dementia and each week more than seventeen hundred people are diagnosed with the disease.

But that figure is set to rise to seven thousand a week, or a total of almost one million by 2050.

Worldwide, 35.6 million people have dementia and there are 7.7 million new cases every year.

"Dementia is the public health challenge of the 21st century," according to Alzheimer's Australia president, Ita Buttrose.

Leading expert, Professor Henry Brodaty from the University of New South Wales, says the disease is a burden on society.

"The numbers are huge and it's a tragedy for their families and it's a tragedy for society," he said.

Alzheimer's disease is the most common type of dementia, accounting for more than half the dementia cases.

Other major forms include vascular dementia; dementia with Lewy bodies (abnormal aggregates of protein that develop inside nerve cells), and a group of diseases that contribute to fronto-temporal dementia (degeneration of the frontal lobe of the brain). The boundaries between different forms of dementia are indistinct and mixed forms often co-exist.

Dementia is difficult to diagnose unless it is a genetic disorder.

Dr Carolyn Orr from Macquarie University Hospital says that with dementia, cognitive function is so impaired that the person is incapable of living independently.

"The first step is to consider whether the patient's symptoms could reflect delirium or depressive pseudo-dementia."

Depression is common in older age groups and has many similar symptoms to dementia. A relatively new term is mild cognitive impairment, a label used to describe people with reduced cognitive abilities but who are able to live independently.

Doctors say many patients feel embarrassed about coming forward with symptoms of memory loss.

"There's a lot of stigma about dementia in general and people are frightened to come forward for a diagnosis," doctors report.

In turn, doctors are often not able to make a diagnosis, or are reluctant to, because they are unsure what can be done for the patient.

"We know there's about a two or three-year gap before first symptoms and diagnosis," Professor Brodaty said.

Mr Brodaty says people should be aware there are many things doctors can do to improve the quality of life of people with dementia.

These include regular exercise; checking blood pressure; maintaining a healthy weight; avoiding obesity and type-2 diabetes.

In addition, diets rich in antioxidants, including eating foods such as fruits and vegetables can help.

Small amounts of alcohol may be protective; though drinking too much may be a risk factor.

Alzheimer's disease is the only kind of neuro-degenerative dementia which has medication to treat it.

The two classes of drugs commonly include cholinesterase inhibitors - useful for cognitive and behavioural symptoms - and glutamate antagonists.

Dr. Orr maintains that using the medications together is moderately effective in delaying the progress of symptoms for a year, though some patients do not respond at all. Medications can also help with symptoms such as depression, agitation or disrupted sleep.

But overall, treatment is temporary and generally only alleviates some of the symptoms for some of the time. Currently there is no way of slowing the progress of the disease or stopping the degenerating of the nerve cells in the brain.

Research and history of the illness

When Alois Alzheimer first described the disease in 1906, plaque had been the prime suspect, triggering nerve damage in the brain. Plaques form when toxic proteins called beta-amyloids clump together.

In 1987, researchers discovered the first gene with mutations found to cause an inherited form of Alzheimer's. There was prospect of a treatment in 1995, when the destructive amyloid protein was successfully removed from mice. The so-called amyloid hypothesis has been the focus of much Alzheimer's research.

Many billions of dollars have been spent researching a cure and recently encouraging results have been achieved but there is still a long way to go.

Recent research suggests intervention needs to start much earlier: dementia begins up to twenty-five years before the first symptoms start to appear.

Other theories are being developed, including looking at inflammation and regeneration in the Alzheimer's brain.

A trial is underway in the United States focusing on families with Alzheimer's to get a better insight into the disease.

Efforts are also continuing to find a drug to delay the onset of dementia with an international trial that involves Australia.

The cost of caring for people with dementia is set to skyrocket with an ageing population.

Currently, it is around six billion dollars or about 1 per cent of GDP. By 2050, it is estimated it will be 2 per cent of GDP.

The Australian Government spent just under twenty two million dollars on dementia research in 2012-13, according to figures from the National Health and Medical Research Council.

Spending on cancer research was more than seven times greater at $162.4 million.

Scientists and advocates say more government funding is desperately needed.

"For far too long this terrible condition has been ignored, downplayed or accepted as a natural part of the ageing process…the truth is, dementia now ranks alongside cancer as one of the greatest enemies of humanity." - David Cameron, British Prime Minister

The End

ACKNOWLEDGEMENTS

Pam Shearer (deceased) For being the inspiration to write this book

Anna Shearer, my wife for her guidance and support

Emma Willmott my daughter (Past GM Alzheimer's Association Queensl
For her help in understanding the subject matter

Kim Krarup for reading yet another of my manuscripts and providing grea
feedback.

David Needam His fourth manuscript as a preview reader

Janet Upcher for another great edit.

Desma Pacito for another great book cover.

BIBLIOGRAPHY

Alzheimer's cure is close: Experts hail new drug breakthrough | Health | News | Daily Expr

About Alzheimer's Disease: Treatment | National Institute on Aging

www.alz.org/national/documents/brochure_ifyouhave_earlystage.pdf

A possible breakthrough in Alzheimer's treatment – Forbes

An Alzheimer's Cure? Not So Fast.. In the Pipeline:

A Caregiver's Personal Story: Getting Into a Dementia Patient's Head – AgingCare.com

The 25 Best Alzheimer's Blogs of 2013

The Annie Scientific: A Short Story about Dementia

Alzheimer's disease real story – Joe and Ethna – Dementia guide – NHS Choices

Marie Marley: When Alzheimer's Is Funny: A Brief Walk on the Light Side of Dementia

Dementia | Come Back Early Today

Funny Senior Moments – Humour, Amusing Pictures and Stories

Unknown Soldiers – a 1918 Draft

Funniest/strangest dementia patient stories – Nursing Humor / Share Jokes

Joke of the day for dementia... | What Makes You Laugh? Support Group | Caring.com

Blood test could detect early signs of dementia, scientists say | Science | The Guardian

Medical laboratory – Wikipedia, the free encyclopedia

Alzheimer's disease – Wikipedia, the free encyclopedia

Alzheimer's disease | NeuRA – Medical Research Institute

Alzheimer's Society – Leading the fight against dementia

Research | Cure Alzheimer's Fund

Funny Emergency Room Stories | DigitalDreamDoor.com

Strange Cases: The Worst of Current Research | Bruce Goldfarb

Eye Test Spots Alzheimer's Before Symptoms

Terry Pratchett – Wikipedia, the free encyclopedia

Things you didn't know about... Being a brain surgeon | Mail Online

www.innovation.org/drug_discovery/objects/pdf/RD_Brochure.pdf

Personal Stories | Frontotemporal Dementia (FTD)

Nursing Homes > Aging & Health A To Z > Health in Aging

Freya Middleton – Freya's Florence tours – Private Tours – About me

Dementia: A looming healthcare disaster – ABC News (Australian Broadcasting Corporation)

SkinCancerNet Article – Melanoma: How It is Staged and Treated